D0615830

THE JUNIOR GREAT BOOKS

DISCUSSION PROGRAM

JUNIOR GREAT BOOKS

A Program of Interpretive Reading
and Discussion

Series Five, Volume Three

EDITED BY
Richard P. Dennis and Edwin P. Moldof

THE GREAT BOOKS FOUNDATION

published and distributed by

THE GREAT BOOKS FOUNDATION
a non-profit corporation
40 East Huron Street
Chicago, Illinois 60611

ACKNOWLEDGEMENTS

The Great Books Foundation wishes to thank the following publishers, authors and literary agencies for permission to reprint the material in this Junior Great Books series:

Heywood Hale Broun for "The Fifty-First Dragon," reprinted from SEEING THINGS AT NIGHT by Heywood Broun.

Doubleday & Company, Inc., for "The Pup," reprinted from SHADOWS AND LIGHT by Anton Chekhov, translated by Miriam Morton, copyright 1968.

Farrar, Straus & Giroux, Inc., New York, for "Charles," from THE LOTTERY by Shirley Jackson, copyright 1948, by Shirley Jackson.

"The Ugly Duckling" and "The Emperor's New Clothes" from IT'S PERFECTLY TRUE AND OTHER STORIES by Hans Christian Andersen, translated by Paul Leyssac, copyright, 1937, by Paul Leyssac; renewed, 1965, by Mary Rehan. These selections are reprinted by special arrangement with Harcourt Brace Jovanovich, Inc.

Macmillan Publishing Co., Inc. for "Maurice's Room," copyright 1966 by Paula Fox.

Harold Matson Company, Inc., New York for "All Summer in a Day," copyright 1954 by Ray Bradbury.

Harold Ober Associates Inc., for "Thank You, M'am," copyright 1958 by Langston Hughes.

CONTENTS

THE WIND IN THE WILLOWS

THE OPEN ROAD

'RATTY,' SAID THE MOLE suddenly, one bright summer morning, 'if you please, I want to ask you a favour.'

The Rat was sitting on the river bank, singing a little song. He had just composed it himself, so he was very taken up with it, and would not pay proper attention to Mole or anything else. Since early morning he had been swimming in the river, in company with his friends the ducks. And when the ducks stood on their heads suddenly, as ducks will, he would dive down and tickle their necks, just under where their chins would be if ducks had chins, till they were forced to come to the surface again in a hurry, spluttering and angry and shaking their feathers at him, for it is impossible to say quite *all* you feel when your head is under water. At last they implored him to go away and attend to his own affairs and leave them to mind theirs. So the Rat went away, and sat on the river bank in the sun, and made up a song about them, which he called

'DUCKS' DITTY.'

All along the backwater,
Through the rushes tall,
Ducks are a-dabbling,
Up tails all!

Ducks' tails, drakes' tails,
Yellow feet a-quiver,
Yellow bills all out of sight
Busy in the river!

Slushy green undergrowth
Where the roach swim—
Here we keep our larder,
Cool and full and dim.

Everyone for what he likes!
We like to be
Heads down, tails up,
Dabbling free!

High in the blue above
Swifts whirl and call—
We are down a-dabbling
Up tails all!

'I don't know that I think so *very* much of that little song, Rat,' observed the Mole cautiously. He was no poet himself and didn't care who knew it; and he had a candid nature.

'Nor don't the ducks neither,' replied the Rat cheerfully. 'They say, "*Why* can't fellows be allowed to do what they like *when* they like and *as* they like, instead of other fellows sitting on banks and watching them all the time and making remarks and poetry and things about them? What *nonsense* it all is!" That's what the ducks say.'

'So it is, so it is,' said the Mole, with great heartiness.

'No, it isn't!' cried the Rat indignantly.

'Well then, it isn't, it isn't,' replied the Mole soothingly. 'But what I wanted to ask you was, won't you take me to call on Mr. Toad? I've heard so much about him, and I do so want to make his acquaintance.'

'Why, certainly,' said the good-natured Rat, jumping to his feet and dismissing poetry from his mind for the day. 'Get the boat out, and we'll paddle up there at once. It's never the wrong time to call on Toad. Early or late he's always the same fellow. Always good-tempered, always glad to see you, always sorry when you go!'

'He must be a very nice animal,' observed the

Mole, as he got into the boat and took the sculls, while the Rat settled himself comfortably in the stern.

'He is indeed the best of animals,' replied Rat. 'So simple, so good-natured, and so affectionate. Perhaps he's not very clever—we can't all be geniuses; and it may be that he is both boastful and conceited. But he has got some great qualities, has Toady.'

Rounding a bend in the river, they came in sight of a handsome, dignified old house of mellowed red brick, with well-kept lawns reaching down to the water's edge.

'There's Toad Hall,' said the Rat; 'and that creek on the left, where the notice-board says, "Private. No landing allowed," leads to his boat-house, where we'll leave the boat. The stables are over there to the right. That's the banqueting-hall you're looking at now—very old, that is. Toad is rather rich, you know, and this is really one of the nicest houses in these parts, though we never admit as much to Toad.'

They glided up the creek, and the Mole shipped his sculls as they passed into the shadow of a large boat-house. Here they saw many handsome boats, slung from the crossbeams or hauled up on a slip, but none in the water; and the place had an unused and a deserted air.

The Rat looked around him. 'I understand,' said he. 'Boating is played out. He's tired of it, and done with it. I wonder what new fad he has taken up now? Come along and let's look him up. We shall hear all about it quite soon enough.'

They disembarked, and strolled across the gay flower-decked lawns in search of Toad, whom they presently happened upon resting in a wicker garden-chair, with a pre-occupied expression of face, and a large map spread out on his knees.

'Hooray!' he cried, jumping up on seeing them, 'this is splendid!' He shook the paws of both of them warmly, never waiting for an introduction to the Mole. 'How *kind* of you!' he went on, dancing round them. 'I was just going to send a boat down the river for you, Ratty, with strict orders that you were to be fetched up here at once, whatever you were doing. I want you badly—both of you. Now what will you take? Come inside and have something! You don't know how lucky it is, your turning up just now!'

'Let's sit quiet a bit, Toady!' said the Rat, throwing himself into an easy chair, while the Mole took another by the side of him and made some civil remark about Toad's 'delightful residence.'

'Finest house on the whole river,' cried Toad boisterously. 'Or anywhere else, for that matter,' he could not help adding.

Here the Rat nudged the Mole. Unfortunately the Toad saw him do it, and turned very red. There was a moment's painful silence. Then Toad burst out laughing. 'All right, Ratty,' he said. 'It's only my way, you know. And it's not such a very bad house, is it? You know you rather like it yourself. Now, look here. Let's be sensible. You are the very animals I wanted. You've got to help me. It's most important!'

'It's about your rowing, I suppose,' said the Rat, with an innocent air. 'You're getting on fairly well, though you splash a good bit still. With a great deal of patience, and any quantity of coaching, you may——'

'O, pooh! boating!' interrupted the Toad, in great disgust. 'Silly boyish amusement. I've given that up *long* ago. Sheer waste of time, that's what it is. It makes me downright sorry to see you fellows, who ought to know better, spending all your energies in that aimless manner. No, I've discovered the real thing, the only genuine occupation for a lifetime. I propose to devote the remainder of mine to it, and can only regret the wasted years that lie behind me, squandered in trivialities. Come with me, dear Ratty, and your amiable friend also, if he will be so very good, just as far as the stable-yard, and you shall see what you shall see!'

He led the way to the stable-yard accordingly,

the Rat following with a most mistrustful expression; and there, drawn out of the coach-house into the open, they saw a gypsy caravan, shining with newness, painted a canary-yellow picked out with green, and red wheels.

'There you are!' cried the Toad, straddling and expanding himself. 'There's real life for you, embodied in that little cart. The open road, the dusty highway, the heath, the common, the hedgerows, the rolling downs! Camps, villages, towns, cities! Here to-day, up and off to somewhere else to-morrow! Travel, change, interest, excitement! The whole world before you, and a horizon that's always changing! And mind! this is the very finest cart of its sort that was ever built, without any exception. Come inside and look at the arrangements. Planned 'em all myself, I did!'

The Mole was tremendously interested and excited, and followed him eagerly up the steps and into the interior of the caravan. The Rat only snorted and thrust his hands deep into his pockets, remaining where he was.

It was indeed very compact and comfortable. Little sleeping bunks—a little table that folded up against the wall—a cooking-stove, lockers, bookshelves, a bird-cage with a bird in it; and pots, pans, jugs and kettles of every size and variety.

'All complete!' said the Toad triumphantly, pulling open a locker. 'You see—biscuits, potted lobster, sardines—everything you can possibly want. Soda-water here—baccy there—letter-paper, bacon, jam, cards and dominoes—you'll find,' he continued, as they descended the steps again, 'you'll find that nothing whatever has been forgotten, when we make our start this afternoon.'

'I beg your pardon,' said the Rat slowly, as he chewed a straw, 'but did I overhear you say something about "*we,*" and "*start,*" and "*this afternoon*"?'

'Now, you dear good old Ratty,' said Toad, imploringly, 'don't begin talking in that stiff and sniffy sort of way, because you know you've *got* to come. I can't possibly manage without you, so please consider it settled, and don't argue—it's the one thing I can't stand. You surely don't mean to stick to your dull fusty old river all your life, and just live in a hole in a bank, and *boat?* I want to show you the world! I'm going to make an *animal* of you, my boy!'

'I don't care,' said the Rat, doggedly. 'I'm not coming, and that's flat. And I *am* going to stick to my old river, *and* live in a hole, *and* boat, as I've always done. And what's more, Mole's going to stick to me and do as I do, aren't you, Mole?'

'Of course I am,' said the Mole, loyally. 'I'll always stick to you, Rat, and what you say is to be—has got to be. All the same, it sounds as if it might have been—well, rather fun, you know!' he added, wistfully. Poor Mole! The Life Adventurous was so new a thing to him, and so thrilling; and this fresh aspect of it was so tempting; and he had fallen in love at first sight with the canary-coloured cart and all its little fitments.

The Rat saw what was passing in his mind, and wavered. He hated disappointing people, and he was fond of the Mole, and would do almost anything to oblige him. Toad was watching both of them closely.

'Come along in, and have some lunch,' he said, diplomatically, 'and we'll talk it over. We needn't decide anything in a hurry. Of course, *I* don't really care. I only want to give pleasure to you fellows. "Live for others!" That's my motto in life.'

During luncheon—which was excellent, of course, as everything at Toad Hall always was—the Toad simply let himself go. Disregarding the Rat, he proceeded to play upon the inexperienced Mole as on a harp. Naturally a voluble animal, and always mastered by his imagination, he painted the prospects of the trip and the joys of the open life and the road-side in such glowing colours that the Mole could hardly sit in his chair for excitement.

Somehow, it soon seemed taken for granted by all three of them that the trip was a settled thing; and the Rat, though still unconvinced in his mind, allowed his good-nature to over-ride his personal objections. He could not bear to disappoint his two friends, who were already deep in schemes and anticipations, planning out each day's separate occupation for several weeks ahead.

When they were quite ready, the now triumphant Toad led his companions to the paddock and set them to capture the old grey horse, who, without having been consulted, and to his own extreme annoyance, had been told off by Toad for the dustiest job in this dusty expedition. He frankly preferred the paddock, and took a deal of catching. Meantime Toad packed the lockers still tighter with necessaries, and hung nosebags, nets of onions, bundles of hay, and baskets from the bottom of the cart. At last the horse was caught and harnessed, and they set off, all talking at once, each animal either trudging by the side of the cart or sitting on the shaft, as the humour took him. It was a golden afternoon. The smell of the dust they kicked up was rich and satisfying; out of thick orchards on either side the road, birds called and whistled to them cheerily; good-natured wayfarers, passing them, gave them 'Good-day,' or stopped to say nice things about their beautiful cart; and rabbits, sitting at their front doors in the hedgerows, held up their forepaws, and said, 'O my! O my! O my!'

Late in the evening, tired and happy and miles from home, they drew up on a remote common far from habitations, turned the horse loose to graze, and ate their simple supper sitting on the grass by the side of the cart. Toad talked big about all he was going to do in the days to come, while stars grew fuller and larger all around them, and a yellow moon, appearing suddenly and silently from nowhere in particular, came to keep them company and listen to their talk. At last they turned in to their little bunks in the cart; and Toad, kicking out his legs, sleepily said, 'Well, good night, you fellows! This is the real life for a gentleman! Talk about your old river!'

'I *don't* talk about my river,' replied the patient Rat. 'You *know* I don't, Toad. But I *think* about it,' he added pathetically, in a lower tone: 'I think about it—all the time!'

The Mole reached out from under his blanket, felt for the Rat's paw in the darkness, and gave it a squeeze. 'I'll do whatever you like, Ratty,' he whispered. 'Shall we run away to-morrow morning, quite early—*very* early—and go back to our dear old hole on the river?'

'No, no, we'll see it out,' whispered back the Rat. 'Thanks awfully, but I ought to stick by Toad till this trip is ended. It wouldn't be safe for him to be left to himself. It won't take very long. His fads never do. Good night!'

The end was indeed nearer than even the Rat suspected.

After so much open air and excitement the Toad slept very soundly, and no amount of shaking could rouse him out of bed next morning. So the Mole and Rat turned to, quietly and manfully, and while the Rat saw to the horse, and lit a fire, and cleaned last night's cups and platters, and got things ready for breakfast, the Mole trudged off to the nearest village, a long way off, for milk and eggs and various necessaries the Toad had, of course, forgotten to provide. The hard work had all been done, and the two animals were resting, thoroughly exhausted, by the time Toad appeared on the scene, fresh and gay, remarking what a pleasant easy life it was they were all leading now, after the cares and worries and fatigues of housekeeping at home.

They had a pleasant ramble that day over grassy downs and along narrow by-lanes, and camped as before, on a common, only this time the two guests took care that Toad should do his fair share of work. In consequence, when the time came for starting next morning, Toad was by no means so rapturous about the simplicity of the primitive life, and indeed attempted to resume his place in his bunk, whence he was hauled by force. Their way lay, as before, across country by narrow lanes, and it was not till the afternoon that they came out on the high-road, their first high-road; and there disaster, fleet and unforeseen, sprang out on them—disaster momentous indeed to their expedition, but simply overwhelming in its effect on the after-career of Toad.

They were strolling along the high-road easily, the Mole by the horse's head, talking to him, since the horse had complained that he was being frightfully left out of it, and nobody considered him in the least; the Toad and the Water Rat walking behind the cart talking together—at least Toad was talking, and Rat was saying at intervals, 'Yes, precisely; and what did *you* say to *him?*'—and thinking all the time of something very different, when far behind them they heard a faint warning hum, like the drone of a distant bee. Glancing back, they saw a small cloud of dust, with a dark centre of energy, advancing on them at incredible speed, while from out the dust a faint 'Poop-poop!' wailed like an uneasy animal in pain. Hardly regarding it, they turned to resume their conversation, when in an instant (as it seemed) the peaceful scene was changed, and with a blast of wind and a whirl of sound that made them jump for the nearest ditch, It was on them! The 'Poop-poop' rang with a brazen shout in their ears, they had a moment's glimpse of an interior of glittering plate-glass and rich morocco and the magnificent motor-car, immense, breath-snatching, passionate, with its pilot tense and hugging his wheel, possessed all earth and air for the fraction of a second, flung an enveloping cloud of dust that blinded and enwrapped them utterly, and then dwindled to a speck in the far distance, changed back into a droning bee once more.

The old grey horse, dreaming, as he plodded along, of his quiet paddock, in a new raw situation such as this simply abandoned himself to his natural emotions. Rearing, plunging, backing steadily, in spite of all the Mole's efforts at his head, and all the Mole's lively language directed at his better feelings, he drove the cart backwards towards the deep ditch at the side of the road. It wavered an instant—then there was a heartrending crash—and the canary-coloured cart, their pride and their joy, lay on its side in the ditch, an irredeemable wreck.

The Rat danced up and down in the road, simply transported with passion. 'You villains!' he shouted, shaking both fists, 'You scoundrels, you highwaymen, you—you—roadhogs!—I'll have the law on you! I'll report you! I'll take you through all the Courts!' His home-sickness had quite slipped away from him, and for the moment he was the skipper of the canary-coloured vessel driven on a shoal by the reckless jockeying of rival mariners, and he was trying to recollect all the fine and biting things he used to say to masters of steam-launches when their wash, as they drove too near the bank, used to flood his parlour-carpet at home.

Toad sat straight down in the middle of the dusty road, his legs stretched out before him, and stared fixedly in the direction of the disappearing motor-car. He breathed short, his face wore a placid satisfied expression, and at intervals he faintly murmured 'Poop-poop!'

The Mole was busy trying to quiet the horse, which he succeeded in doing after a time. Then he went to look at the cart, on its side in the ditch. It was indeed a sorry sight. Panels and windows smashed, axles hopelessly bent, one wheel off, sardine-tins scattered over the wide world, and the bird in the bird-cage sobbing pitifully and calling to be let out.

The Rat came to help him, but their united efforts were not sufficient to right the cart. 'Hi!

Toad!' they cried. 'Come and bear a hand, can't you!'

The Toad never answered a word, or budged from his seat in the road; so they went to see what was the matter with him. They found him in a sort of a trance, a happy smile on his face, his eyes still fixed on the dusty wake of their destroyer. At intervals he was still heard to murmur 'Poop-poop!'

The Rat shook him by the shoulder. 'Are you coming to help us, Toad?' he demanded sternly.

'Glorious, stirring sight!' murmured Toad, never offering to move. 'The poetry of motion! The *real* way to travel! The *only* way to travel! Here to-day—in next week to-morrow! Villages skipped, towns and cities jumped—always somebody else's horizon! O bliss! O poop-poop! O my! O my!'

'O *stop* being an ass, Toad!' cried the Mole despairingly.

'And to think I never *knew!*' went on the Toad in a dreamy monotone. 'All those wasted years that lie behind me, I never knew, never even *dreamt!* But *now*—but now that I know, now that I fully realise! O what a flowery track lies spread before me, henceforth! What dust-clouds shall spring up behind me as I speed on my reckless way! What carts I shall fling carelessly into the ditch in the wake of my magnificent onset! Horrid little carts—common carts—canary-coloured carts!'

'What are we to do with him?' asked the Mole of the Water Rat.

'Nothing at all,' replied the Rat firmly. 'Because there is really nothing to be done. You see, I know him from of old. He is now possessed. He has got a new craze, and it always takes him that way, in its first stage. He'll continue like that for days now, like an animal walking in a happy dream, quite useless for all practical purposes. Never mind him. Let's go and see what there is to be done about the cart.'

A careful inspection showed them that, even if they succeeded in righting it by themselves, the cart would travel no longer. The axles were in a hopeless state, and the missing wheel was shattered into pieces.

The Rat knotted the horse's reins over his back and took him by the head, carrying the bird-cage and its hysterical occupant in the other hand. 'Come on!' he said grimly to the Mole. 'It's five or six miles to the nearest town, and we shall just have to walk it. The sooner we make the start the better.'

'But what about Toad?' asked the Mole anxiously, as they set off together. 'We can't leave him here, sitting in the middle of the road by himself, in the distracted state he's in! It's not safe. Supposing another Thing were to come along?'

'O, *bother* Toad,' said the Rat savagely; 'I've done with him!'

They had not proceeded very far on their way, however, when there was a pattering of feet behind them, and Toad caught them up and thrust a paw inside the elbow of each of them; still breathing short and staring into vacancy.

'Now, look here, Toad!' said the Rat sharply: 'as soon as we get to the town, you'll have to go straight to the police-station, and see if they know anything about that motor-car and who it belongs to, and lodge a complaint against it. And then you'll have to go to a blacksmith's or a wheel-wright's and arrange for the cart to be fetched and mended and put to rights. It'll take time, but it's not quite a hopeless smash. Meanwhile, the Mole and I will go to an inn and find comfortable rooms where we can stay till the cart's ready, and till your nerves have recovered their shock.'

'Police-station! Complaint!' murmured Toad dreamily. 'Me *complain* of that beautiful, that heav-enly vision that has been vouchsafed me! *Mend* the *cart!* I've done with carts for ever. I never want to see the cart, or to hear of it, again. O, Ratty! You can't think how obliged I am to you for consenting to come on this trip! I wouldn't have gone without you, and then I might never have seen that—that swan, that sunbeam, that thunderbolt! I might never have heard that entrancing sound, or smelt that bewitching smell! I owe it all to you, my best of friends!'

The Rat turned from him in despair. 'You see what it is?' he said to the Mole, addressing him across Toad's head: 'He's quite hopeless. I give it up—when we get to the town we'll go to the railway station, and with luck we may pick up a train there that'll get us back to River Bank to-night. And if ever you catch me going a-pleasuring with this provoking animal again!'—He snorted, and during the rest of that weary trudge addressed his remarks exclusively to Mole.

On reaching the town they went straight to the station and deposited Toad in the second-class waiting-room, giving a porter twopence to keep a strict eye on him. They then left the horse at an inn stable, and gave what directions they could about the cart and its contents. Eventually, a slow train having landed them at a station not very far from Toad Hall, they escorted the spell-bound, sleep-walking Toad to his door, put him inside it, and instructed his housekeeper to feed him, undress him, and put him to bed. Then they got out their boat from the boat-house, sculled down the river home, and at a very late hour sat down to supper in their own cosy riverside parlour, to the Rat's great joy and contentment.

The following evening the Mole, who had risen late and taken things very easy all day, was sitting on the bank fishing, when the Rat, who had been looking up his friends and gossiping, came strolling along to find him. 'Heard the news?' he said. 'There's nothing else being talked about, all along the river bank. Toad went up to Town by an early train this morning. And he has ordered a large and very expensive motor-car.'

MR. TOAD

It was a bright morning in the early part of summer; the river had resumed its wonted banks and its accustomed pace, and a hot sun seemed to be pulling everything green and bushy and spiky up out of the earth towards him, as if by strings. The Mole and the Water Rat had been up since dawn, very busy on matters connected with boats and the opening of the boating season; painting and varnishing, mending paddles, repairing cushions, hunting for missing boat-hooks, and so on; and were finishing breakfast in their little parlour and eagerly discussing their plans for the day, when a heavy knock sounded at the door.

'Bother!' said the Rat, all over egg. 'See who it is, Mole, like a good chap, since you've finished.'

The Mole went to attend the summons, and the Rat heard him utter a cry of surprise. Then he flung the parlour door open, and announced with much importance, 'Mr. Badger!'

This was a wonderful thing, indeed, that the Badger should pay a formal call on them, or indeed on anybody. He generally had to be caught, if you wanted him badly, as he slipped quietly along a hedgerow of an early morning or a late evening, or else hunted up in his own house in the middle of the Woods, which was a serious undertaking.

The Badger strode heavily into the room, and stood looking at the two animals with an expression full of seriousness. The Rat let his egg-spoon fall on the table-cloth, and sat open-mouthed.

'The hour has come!' said the Badger at last with great solemnity.

'What hour?' asked the Rat uneasily, glancing at the clock on the mantelpiece.

'*Whose* hour, you should rather say,' replied the Badger. 'Why, Toad's hour! The hour of Toad! I said I would take him in hand as soon as the winter was well over, and I'm going to take him in hand to-day!'

'Toad's hour, of course!' cried the Mole delightedly. 'Hooray! I remember now! *We'll* teach him to be a sensible Toad!'

'This very morning,' continued the Badger, taking an arm-chair, 'as I learnt last night from a trustworthy source, another new and exceptionally powerful motor-car will arrive at Toad Hall on approval or return. At this very moment, perhaps, Toad is busy arraying himself in those singularly hideous habiliments so dear to him, which transform him from a (comparatively) good-looking Toad into an Object which throws any decent-minded animal that comes across it into a violent fit. We must be up and doing, ere it is too late. You two animals will accompany me instantly to Toad Hall, and the work of rescue shall be accomplished.'

'Right you are!' cried the Rat, starting up. 'We'll rescue the poor unhappy animal! We'll convert him! He'll be the most converted Toad that ever was before we've done with him!'

They set off up the road on their mission of mercy, Badger leading the way. Animals when in company walk in a proper and sensible manner, in single file, instead of sprawling all across the road and being of no use or support to each other in case of sudden trouble or danger.

They reached the carriage-drive of Toad Hall to find, as the Badger had anticipated, a shiny new motor-car, of great size, painted a bright red (Toad's favourite colour), standing in front of the house. As they neared the door it was flung open, and Mr. Toad, arrayed in goggles, cap, gaiters, and enormous overcoat, came swaggering down the steps, drawing on his gauntleted gloves.

'Hullo! come on, you fellows!' he cried cheerfully

on catching sight of them. 'You're just in time to come with me for a jolly—to come for a jolly—for a—er—jolly——'

His hearty accents faltered and fell away as he noticed the stern unbending look on the countenances of his silent friends, and his invitation remained unfinished.

The Badger strode up the steps. 'Take him inside,' he said sternly to his companions. Then, as Toad was hustled through the door, struggling and protesting, he turned to the *chauffeur* in charge of the new motor-car.

'I'm afraid you won't be wanted to-day,' he said. 'Mr. Toad has changed his mind. He will not require the car. Please understand that this is final. You needn't wait.' Then he followed the others inside and shut the door.

'Now then!' he said to the Toad, when the four of them stood together in the Hall, 'first of all, take those ridiculous things off!'

'Shan't!' replied Toad, with great spirit. 'What is the meaning of this gross outrage? I demand an instant explanation.'

'Take them off him, then, you two,' ordered the Badger briefly.

They had to lay Toad out on the floor, kicking and calling all sorts of names, before they could get to work properly. Then the Rat sat on him, and the

Mole got his motor-clothes off him bit by bit, and they stood him up on his legs again. A good deal of his blustering spirit seemed to have evaporated with the removal of his fine panoply. Now that he was merely Toad, and no longer the Terror of the Highway, he giggled feebly and looked from one to the other appealingly, seeming quite to understand the situation.

'You knew it must come to this, sooner or later, Toad,' the Badger explained severely. 'You've disregarded all the warnings we've given you, you've gone on squandering the money your father left you, and you're getting us animals a bad name in the district by your furious driving and your smashes and your rows with the police. Independence is all very well, but we animals never allow our friends to make fools of themselves beyond a certain limit; and that limit you've reached. Now, you're a good fellow in many respects, and I don't want to be too hard on you. I'll make one more effort to bring you to reason. You will come with me into the smoking-room, and there you will hear some facts about yourself; and we'll see whether you come out of that room the same Toad that you went in.'

He took Toad firmly by the arm, led him into the smoking-room, and closed the door behind him.

'*That's* no good!' said the Rat contemptuously.

'*Talking* to Toad'll never cure him. He'll *say* anything.'

They made themselves comfortable in arm-chairs and waited patiently. Through the closed door they could just hear the long continuous drone of the Badger's voice, rising and falling in waves of oratory; and presently they noticed that the sermon began to be punctuated at intervals by long-drawn sobs, evidently proceeding from the bosom of Toad, who was a soft-hearted and affectionate fellow, very easily converted—for the time being—to any point of view.

After some three-quarters of an hour the door opened, and the Badger reappeared, solemnly leading by the paw a very limp and dejected Toad. His skin hung baggily about him, his legs wobbled, and his cheeks were furrowed by the tears so plentifully called forth by the Badger's moving discourse.

'Sit down there, Toad,' said the Badger kindly, pointing to a chair. 'My friends,' he went on, 'I am pleased to inform you that Toad has at last seen the error of his ways. He is truly sorry for his misguided conduct in the past, and he has undertaken to give up motor-cars entirely and for ever. I have his solemn promise to that effect.'

'That is very good news,' said the Mole gravely.

'Very good news indeed,' observed the Rat dubiously, 'if only—*if* only——'

He was looking very hard at Toad as he said this, and could not help thinking he perceived something vaguely resembling a twinkle in that animal's still sorrowful eye.

'There's only one thing more to be done,' continued the gratified Badger. 'Toad, I want you solemnly to repeat, before your friends here, what you fully admitted to me in the smoking-room just now. First, you are sorry for what you've done, and you see the folly of it all?'

There was a long, long pause. Toad looked desperately this way and that, while the other animals waited in grave silence. At last he spoke.

'No!' he said, a little sullenly, but stoutly; 'I'm *not* sorry. And it wasn't folly at all! It was simply glorious!'

'What?' cried the Badger, greatly scandalised. 'You backsliding animal, didn't you tell me just now, in there——'

'Oh, yes, yes, in *there,*' said Toad impatiently. 'I'd have said anything in *there*. You're so eloquent, dear Badger, and so moving, and so convincing, and put all your points so frightfully well—you can do what you like with me in *there,* and you know it. But I've been searching my mind since, and going over things in it, and I find that I'm not a bit sorry or repentant really, so it's no earthly good saying I am; now, is it?'

'Then you don't promise,' said the Badger, 'never to touch a motor-car again?'

'Certainly not!' replied Toad emphatically. 'On the contrary, I faithfully promise that the very first motor-car I see, poop-poop! off I go in it!'

'Told you so, didn't I?' observed the Rat to the Mole.

'Very well, then,' said the Badger firmly, rising to his feet. 'Since you won't yield to persuasion, we'll try what force can do. I feared it would come to this all along. You've often asked us three to come and stay with you, Toad, in this handsome house of yours; well, now we're going to. When we've converted you to a proper point of view we may quit, but not before. Take him upstairs, you two, and lock him up in his bedroom, while we arrange matters between ourselves.'

'It's for your own good, Toady, you know,' said the Rat kindly, as Toad, kicking and struggling, was hauled up the stairs by his two faithful friends. 'Think what fun we shall all have together, just as we used to, when you've quite got over this—this painful attack of yours!'

'We'll take great care of everything for you till you're well, Toad,' said the Mole; 'and we'll see your money isn't wasted, as it has been.'

'No more of those regrettable incidents with the

police, Toad,' said the Rat, as they thrust him into his bedroom.

'And no more weeks in hospital, being ordered about by female nurses, Toad,' added the Mole, turning the key on him.

They descended the stair, Toad shouting abuse at them through the keyhole; and the three friends then met in conference on the situation.

'It's going to be a tedious business,' said the Badger, sighing. 'I've never seen Toad so determined. However, we will see it out. He must never be left an instant unguarded. We shall have to take it in turns to be with him, till the poison has worked itself out of his system.'

They arranged watches accordingly. Each animal took it in turns to sleep in Toad's room at night, and they divided the day up between them. At first Toad was undoubtedly very trying to his careful guardians. When his violent paroxysms possessed him he would arrange bedroom chairs in rude resemblance of a motor-car and would crouch on the foremost of them, bent forward and staring fixedly ahead, making uncouth and ghastly noises, till the climax was reached, when, turning a complete somersault, he would lie prostrate amidst the ruins of the chairs, apparently completely satisfied for the moment. As time passed, however, these painful seizures grew gradually less frequent, and his friends strove to divert his mind into fresh channels. But his interest in other matters did not seem to revive, and he grew apparently languid and depressed.

One fine morning the Rat, whose turn it was to go on duty, went upstairs to relieve Badger, whom he found fidgeting to be off and stretch his legs in a long ramble round his wood and down his earths and burrows. 'Toad's still in bed,' he told the Rat, outside the door. 'Can't get much out of him, except, "O leave him alone, he wants nothing, perhaps he'll be better presently, it may pass off in time, don't be unduly anxious," and so on. Now, you look out, Rat! When Toad's quiet and submissive, and playing at being the hero of a Sunday-school prize, then he's at his artfullest. There's sure to be something up. I know him. Well, now, I must be off.'

'How are you to-day, old chap?' inquired the Rat cheerfully, as he approached Toad's bedside.

He had to wait some minutes for an answer. At last a feeble voice replied, 'Thank you so much, dear Ratty! So good of you to inquire! But first tell me how you are yourself, and the excellent Mole?'

'O, *we're* all right,' replied the Rat. 'Mole,' he

added incautiously, 'is going out for a run round with Badger. They'll be out till luncheon time, so you and I will spend a pleasant morning together, and I'll do my best to amuse you. Now jump up, there's a good fellow, and don't lie moping there on a fine morning like this!'

'Dear, kind Rat,' murmured Toad, 'how little you realise my condition, and how very far I am from "jumping up now"—if ever! But do not trouble about me. I hate being a burden to my friends, and I do not expect to be one much longer. Indeed, I almost hope not.'

'Well, I hope not, too,' said the Rat heartily. 'You've been a fine bother to us all this time, and I'm glad to hear it's going to stop. And in weather like this, and the boating season just beginning! It's too bad of you, Toad! It isn't the trouble we mind, but you're making us miss such an awful lot.'

'I'm afraid it *is* the trouble you mind, though,' replied the Toad languidly. 'I can quite understand it. It's natural enough. You're tired of bothering about me. I mustn't ask you to do anything further. I'm a nuisance, I know.'

'You are, indeed,' said the Rat. 'But I tell you, I'd take any trouble on earth for you, if only you'd be a sensible animal.'

'If I thought that, Ratty,' murmured Toad, more

feebly than ever, 'then I would beg you—for the last time, probably—to step round to the village as quickly as possible—even now it may be too late—and fetch the doctor. But don't you bother. It's only a trouble, and perhaps we may as well let things take their course.'

'Why, what do you want a doctor for?' inquired the Rat, coming closer and examining him. He certainly lay very still and flat, and his voice was weaker and his manner much changed.

'Surely you have noticed of late——' murmured Toad. 'But, no—why should you? Noticing things is only a trouble. To-morrow, indeed, you may be saying to yourself, "O, if only I had noticed sooner! If only I had done something!" But no; it's a trouble. Never mind—forget that I asked.'

'Look here, old man,' said the Rat, beginning to get rather alarmed, 'of course I'll fetch a doctor to you, if you really think you want him. But you can hardly be bad enough for that yet. Let's talk about something else.'

'I fear, dear friend,' said Toad, with a sad smile, 'that "talk" can do little in a case like this—or doctors either, for that matter; still, one must grasp at the slightest straw. And, by the way—while you are about it—I *hate* to give you additional trouble, but I happen to remember that you will pass the door—would you mind at the same time asking the lawyer to step up? It would be a convenience to me, and there are moments—perhaps I should say there is *a* moment—when one must face disagreeable tasks, at whatever cost to exhausted nature!'

'A lawyer! O, he must be really bad!' the affrighted Rat said to himself, as he hurried from the room, not forgetting, however, to lock the door carefully behind him.

Outside, he stopped to consider. The other two were far away, and he had not one to consult.

'It's best to be on the safe side,' he said, on reflection. 'I've known Toad fancy himself frightfully bad before, without the slightest reason; but I've never heard him ask for a lawyer! If there's nothing really the matter, the doctor will tell him he's an old ass, and cheer him up; and that will be something gained. I'd better humour him and go; it won't take very long.' So he ran off to the village on his errand of mercy.

The Toad, who had hopped lightly out of bed as soon as he heard the key turned in the lock watched him eagerly from the window till he disappeared down the carriage-drive. Then, laughing heartily, he dressed as quickly as possible in the smartest suit he could lay hands on at the moment, filled his pockets with cash which he took from a small drawer in the dressing-table, and next, knotting the sheets from his bed together and tying one end of the improvised rope round the central mullion of the handsome Tudor window which formed such a feature of his bedroom, he scrambled out, slid lightly to the ground, and, taking the opposite direction to the Rat, marched off light-heartedly, whistling a merry tune.

It was a gloomy luncheon for Rat when the Badger and the Mole at length returned, and he had to face them at table with his pitiful and unconvincing story. The Badger's caustic, not to say brutal, remarks may be imagined, and therefore passed over; but it was painful to the Rat that even the Mole, though he took his friend's side as far as possible, could not help saying, 'You've been a bit of a duffer this time, Ratty! Toad, too, of all animals!'

'He did it awfully well,' said the crestfallen Rat.

'He did *you* awfully well!' rejoined the Badger hotly. 'However, talking won't mend matters. He's got clear away for the time, that's certain; and the worst of it is, he'll be so conceited with what he'll think is his cleverness that he may commit any folly. One comfort is, we're free now, and needn't waste any more of our precious time doing sentry-go. But we'd better continue to sleep at Toad Hall for a while longer. Toad may be brought back at any moment—on a stretcher, or between two policemen.'

So spoke the Badger, not knowing what the future held in store, or how much water, and of how turbid a character, was to run under bridges before Toad should sit at ease again in his ancestral Hall.

Meanwhile, Toad, gay and irresponsible, was walking briskly along the high road, some miles from home. At first he had taken by-paths, and crossed many fields, and changed his course several times, in case of pursuit; but now, feeling by this time safe from recapture, and the sun smiling brightly on him, and all Nature joining in a chorus of approval to the song of self-praise that his own heart was singing to him, he almost danced along the road in his satisfaction and conceit.

'Smart piece of work that!' he remarked to himself chuckling. 'Brain against brute force—and brain came out on the top—as it's bound to do. Poor old Ratty! My! won't he catch it when the Badger gets back! A worthy fellow, Ratty, with many good qualities, but very little intelligence and absolutely no education. I must take him in hand some day, and see if I can make something of him.'

Filled full of conceited thoughts such as these he strode along, his head in the air, till he reached a little town, where the sign of 'The Red Lion,' swinging across the road half-way down the main street, reminded him that he had not breakfasted that day, and that he was exceedingly hungry after his long walk. He marched into the Inn, ordered the best luncheon that could be provided at so short a notice, and sat down to eat it in the coffee-room.

He was about half-way through his meal when an only too familiar sound, approaching down the street, made him start and fall a trembling all over. The poop-poop! drew nearer and nearer, the car could be heard to turn into the inn-yard and come to a stop, and Toad had to hold on to the leg of the table to conceal his over-mastering emotion. Presently the party entered the coffee-room, hungry, talkative, and gay, voluble on their experiences of the morning and the merits of the chariot that had brought them along so well. Toad listened eagerly, all ears, for a time; at last he could stand it no longer. He slipped out of the room quietly, paid his bill at the bar, and as soon as he got outside sauntered round quietly to the inn-yard. 'There cannot be any harm,' he said to himself, 'in my only just *looking* at it!'

The car stood in the middle of the yard, quite unattended, the stable-helps and other hangers-on being all at their dinner. Toad walked slowly round it, inspecting, criticising, musing deeply.

'I wonder,' he said to himself presently, 'I wonder if this sort of car *starts* easily?'

Next moment, hardly knowing how it came about, he found he had hold of the handle and was turning it. As the familiar sound broke forth, the old passion seized on Toad and completely mastered him, body and soul. As if in a dream he found himself, somehow, seated in the driver's seat; as if in a dream, he pulled the lever and swung the car round the yard and out through the archway; and, as if in a dream, all sense of right and wrong, all fear of obvious consequences, seemed temporarily suspended. He increased his pace, and as the car devoured the street and leapt forth on the high road through the open country, he was only conscious that he was Toad once more, Toad at his best and highest, Toad the terror, the traffic-queller, the Lord of the lone trail, before whom all must give way or be smitten into nothingness and everlasting night. He chanted as he flew, and the car responded with sonorous drone; the miles were eaten up under him as he sped he knew not whither, fulfilling his instincts, living his hour, reckless of what might come to him.

* * *

'To my mind,' observed the Chairman of the Bench of Magistrates cheerfully, 'the *only* difficulty that presents itself in this otherwise very clear case is, how we can possibly make it sufficiently hot for the incorrigible rogue and hardened ruffian whom we see cowering in the dock before us. Let me see: he has been found guilty, on the clearest evidence, first, of stealing a valuable motor-car; secondly, of driving to the public danger; and, thirdly, of gross impertinence to the rural police. Mr. Clerk, will you tell us, please, what is the very stiffest penalty we can impose for each of these offences? Without, of course, giving the prisoner the benefit of any doubt, because there isn't any.'

The Clerk scratched his nose with his pen. 'Some people would consider,' he observed, 'that stealing the motor-car was the worst offence; and so it is. But cheeking the police undoubtedly carries the severest penalty; and so it ought. Supposing you were to say twelve months for the theft, which is mild; and three years for the furious driving, which is lenient; and fifteen years for the cheek, which was pretty bad sort of cheek, judging by what we've heard from the witness-box, even if you only believe one-tenth part of what you heard, and I never believe more myself—those figures, if added together correctly, tot up to nineteen years——'

'First-rate!' said the Chairman.

'—So you had better make it a round twenty years and be on the safe side,' concluded the Clerk.

'An excellent suggestion!' said the Chairman approvingly. 'Prisoner! Pull yourself together and try and stand up straight. It's going to be twenty years for you this time. And mind, if you appear before us again, upon any charge whatever, we shall have to deal with you very seriously!'

Then the brutal minions of the law fell upon the hapless Toad; loaded him with chains, and dragged him from the Court House, shrieking, praying, protesting; across the market-place, where the playful populace, always as severe upon detected crime as they are sympathetic and helpful when one is merely 'wanted,' assailed him with jeers, carrots, and popular catch-words; past hooting school children, their innocent faces lit up with the pleasure they ever derive from the sight of a gentleman in difficulties; across the hollow-sounding drawbridge, below the spiky portcullis, under the frowning archway of the grim old castle, whose ancient towers soared high overhead; past guardrooms full of grinning soldiery off duty, past sentries who coughed in a horrid, sarcastic way, because that is as much as a sentry on his post dare do to show his contempt and abhorrence of crime; up time-worn winding stairs, past men-at-arms in casquet and corselet of steel, darting threatening looks through their vizards; across courtyards, where mastiffs strained at their leash and pawed the air to get at him; past ancient warders, their halberds leant against the wall, dozing over a pasty and a flagon of brown ale; on and on, past the rack-chamber and the thumbscrew-room, past the turning that led to the private scaffold, till they reached the door of the grimmest dungeon that lay in the heart of the innermost keep. There at last they paused, where an ancient gaoler sat fingering a bunch of mighty keys.

'Oddsbodikins!' said the sergeant of police, taking off his helmet and wiping his forehead. 'Rouse thee, old loon, and take over from us this vile Toad, a criminal of deepest guilt and matchless artfulness and resource. Watch and ward him with all thy skill; and mark thee well, greybeard, should aught untoward befall, thy old head shall answer for his—and a murrain on both of them!'

The gaoler nodded grimly, laying his withered hand on the shoulder of the miserable Toad. The rusty key creaked in the lock, the great door clanged behind them; and Toad was a helpless prisoner in the remotest dungeon of the best-guarded keep of the stoutest castle in all the length and breadth of Merry England.

TOAD'S ADVENTURES

When Toad found himself immured in a dank and noisome dungeon, and knew that all the grim darkness of a medieval fortress lay between him and the outer world of sunshine and well-metalled high roads where he had lately been so happy, disporting himself as if he had bought up every road in England, he flung himself at full length on the floor, and shed bitter tears, and abandoned himself to dark despair. 'This is the end of everything' (he said), 'at least it is the end of the career of Toad, which is the same thing; the popular and handsome Toad, the rich and hospitable Toad, the Toad so free and careless and debonair! How can I hope to be ever set at large again' (he said), 'who have been imprisoned so justly for stealing so handsome a motor-car in such an audacious manner, and for such lurid and imaginative cheek, bestowed upon such a number of fat, red-faced policemen!' (Here his sobs choked him.) 'Stupid animal that I was' (he said), 'now I must languish in this dungeon, till people who were proud to say they knew me, have forgotten the very name of Toad! O wise old Badger!' (he said), 'O clever, intelligent Rat and sensible Mole! What sound judgments, what a knowledge of men and matters you possess! O unhappy and forsaken Toad!' With lamentations such as these he passed his days and nights for several weeks, refusing his meals or intermediate light refreshments, though the grim and ancient gaoler, knowing that Toad's pockets were well lined, frequently pointed out that many comforts, and indeed luxuries, could by arrangement be sent in—at a price—from outside.

Now the gaoler had a daughter, a pleasant wench and good-hearted, who assisted her father in the lighter duties of his post. She was particularly fond of animals, and, besides her canary, whose cage hung on a nail in the massive wall of the keep by day, to the great annoyance of prisoners who relished an after-dinner nap, and was shrouded in an antimacassar on the parlour table at night, she kept several piebald mice and a restless revolving squirrel. This kindhearted girl, pitying the misery of Toad, said to her father one day, 'Father! I can't bear to see that poor beast so unhappy, and getting so thin! You let me have the managing of him. You know how fond of animals I am. I'll make him eat from my hand, and sit up, and do all sorts of things.'

Her father replied that she could do what she liked with him. He was tired of Toad, and his sulks and his airs and his meanness. So that day she went on her errand of mercy, and knocked at the door of Toad's cell.

'Now, cheer up, Toad,' she said, coaxingly, on entering, 'and sit up and dry your eyes and be a sensible animal. And do try and eat a bit of dinner. See, I've brought you some of mine, hot from the oven!"

It was bubble-and-squeak, between two plates, and its fragrance filled the narrow cell. The penetrating smell of cabbage reached the nose of Toad as he lay prostrate in his misery on the floor, and gave him the idea for a moment that perhaps life was not such a blank and desperate thing as he had imagined. But still he wailed, and kicked with his legs, and refused to be comforted. So the wise girl retired for the time, but, of course, a good deal of the smell of hot cabbage remained behind, as it will do, and Toad, between his sobs, sniffed and reflected, and gradually began to think new and inspiring thoughts: of chivalry, and poetry, and deeds still to be done; of broad meadows, and cattle browsing in them, raked by sun and wind; of kitchen-gardens, and straight herb-borders, and warm snap-dragon beset by bees; and of the comforting clink of dishes set down on the table at Toad Hall, and the scrape of chair-legs on the floor as every one pulled himself close up to his work. The air of the narrow cell took a rosy tinge; he began to think of his friends, and how they would surely be able to do something; of lawyers, and how they would have enjoyed his case, and what an ass he had been not to get in a few; and lastly, he thought of his own great cleverness and resource, and all that he was capable of if he only gave his great mind to it; and the cure was almost complete.

When the girl returned, some hours later, she carried a tray, with a cup of fragrant tea steaming on it; and a plate piled up with very hot buttered toast, cut thick, very brown on both sides, with the butter running through the holes in it in great golden drops, like honey from the honeycomb. The smell of that buttered toast simply talked to Toad, and with no uncertain voice; talked of warm kitchens, of breakfasts on bright frosty mornings, of cosy parlour firesides on winter evenings, when one's ramble was over and slippered feet were propped on the fender; of the purring of contented cats, and the twitter of sleepy canaries. Toad sat up on end once more, dried his eyes, sipped his tea and munched his toast, and soon began talking freely about himself, and the house he lived in, and his doings there, and how important he was, and what a lot his friends thought of him.

The gaoler's daughter saw that the topic was doing him as much good as the tea, as indeed it was, and encouraged him to go on.

'Tell me about Toad Hall,' said she. 'It sounds beautiful.'

'Toad Hall,' said the Toad proudly, 'is an eligible self-contained gentleman's residence, very unique; dating in part from the fourteenth century, but replete with every modern convenience. Up-to-date sanitation. Five minutes from church, post-office, and golf-links. Suitable for——'

'Bless the animal,' said the girl, laughing, 'I don't want to *take* it. Tell me something *real* about it. But first wait till I fetch you some more tea and toast.'

She tripped away, and presently returned with a fresh trayful; and Toad, pitching into the toast with avidity, his spirits quite restored to their usual level, told her about the boat-house, and the fish-pond, and the old walled kitchen-garden; and about the pig-styes, and the stables, and the pigeon-house, and the hen-house; and about the dairy, and the wash-house, and the china-cupboards, and the linen-presses (she liked that bit especially); and about the banqueting-hall, and the fun they had there when the other animals were gathered round the table and Toad was at his best, singing songs, telling stories, carrying on generally. Then she wanted to know about his animal-friends, and was very interested in all he had to tell her about them and how they lived, and what they did to pass their time. Of course, she did not say she was fond of animals as *pets,* because she had the sense to see that Toad would be extremely offended. When she said good night, having filled his water-jug and shaken up his straw for him, Toad was very much the same sanguine, self-satisfied animal that he had been of old. He sang a little song or two, of the sort he used to sing at his dinner-parties, curled himself up in the straw, and had an excellent night's rest and the pleasantest of dreams.

They had many interesting talks together, after that, as the dreary days went on; and the gaoler's daughter grew very sorry for Toad, and thought it a great shame that a poor little animal should be locked up in prison for what seemed to her a very trivial offence. Toad, of course, in his vanity, thought that her interest in him proceeded from a growing tenderness; and he could not help half-regretting that the social gulf between them was so very wide, for she was a comely lass, and evidently admired him very much.

One morning the girl was very thoughtful, and

answered at random, and did not seem to Toad to be paying proper attention to his witty sayings and sparkling comments.

'Toad,' she said presently, 'just listen, please. I have an aunt who is a washerwoman.'

'There, there,' said Toad, graciously and affably, 'never mind; think no more about it. *I* have several aunts who *ought* to be washerwomen.'

'Do be quiet a minute, Toad,' said the girl. 'You talk too much, that's your chief fault, and I'm trying to think, and you hurt my head. As I said, I have an aunt who is a washerwoman; she does the washing for all the prisoners in this castle—we try to keep any paying business of that sort in the family, you understand. She takes out the washing on Monday morning, and brings it in on Friday evening. This is a Thursday. Now, this is what occurs to me: you're very rich—at least you're always telling me so—and she's very poor. A few pounds wouldn't make any difference to you, and it would mean a lot to her. Now, I think if she were properly approached—squared, I believe is the word you animals use—you could come to some arrangement by which she would let you have her dress and bonnet and so on, and you could escape from the castle as the official washerwoman. You're very alike in many respects—particularly about the figure.'

'We're *not,'* said the Toad in a huff. 'I have a very elegant figure—for what I am.'

'So has my aunt,' replied the girl, 'for what *she* is. But have it your own way. You horrid, proud, ungrateful animal, when I'm sorry for you, and trying to help you!'

'Yes, yes, that's all right; thank you very much indeed,' said the Toad hurriedly. 'But look here! you wouldn't surely have Mr. Toad, of Toad Hall, going about the country disguised as a washer-woman!'

'Then you can stop here as a Toad,' replied the girl with much spirit. 'I suppose you want to go off in a coach-and-four!'

Honest Toad was always ready to admit himself in the wrong. 'You are a good, kind, clever girl,' he said, 'and I am indeed a proud and a stupid toad. Introduce me to your worthy aunt, if you will be so kind, and I have no doubt that the excellent lady and I will be able to arrange terms satisfactory to both parties.'

Next evening the girl ushered her aunt into Toad's cell, bearing his week's washing pinned up in a towel. The old lady had been prepared beforehand for the interview, and the sight of certain gold sovereigns that Toad had thoughtfully placed on the table in full view practically completed the matter and left little further to discuss. In return for his cash, Toad received a cotton print gown, an apron, a shawl, and a rusty black bonnet; the only stipulation the old lady made being that she should be gagged and bound and dumped down in a corner. By this not very convincing artifice, she explained, aided by picturesque fiction which she could supply herself, she hoped to retain her situation, in spite of the suspicious appearance of things.

Toad was delighted with the suggestion. It would enable him to leave the prison in some style, and with his reputation for being a desperate and dangerous fellow untarnished; and he readily helped the gaoler's daughter to make her aunt appear as much as possible the victim of circumstances over which she had no control.

'Now it's your turn, Toad,' said the girl. 'Take off that coat and waistcoat of yours; you're fat enough as it is.'

Shaking with laughter, she proceeded to 'hook-and-eye' him into the cotton print gown, arranged the shawl with a professional fold, and tied the strings of the rusty bonnet under his chin.

'You're the very image of her,' she giggled, 'only

I'm sure you never looked half so respectable in all your life before. Now, good-bye, Toad, and good luck. Go straight down the way you came up; and if any one says anything to you, as they probably will, being but men, you can chaff back a bit, of course, but remember you're a widow woman, quite alone in the world, with a character to lose.'

With a quaking heart, but as firm a footstep as he could command, Toad set forth cautiously on what seemed to be a most hare-brained and hazardous undertaking; but he was soon agreeably surprised to find how easy everything was made for him, and a little humbled at the thought that both his popularity, and the sex that seemed to inspire it, were really another's. The washerwoman's squat figure in its familiar cotton print seemed a passport for every barred door and grim gateway; even when he hesitated, uncertain as to the right turning to take, he found himself helped out of his difficulty by the warder at the next gate, anxious to be off to his tea, summoning him to come along sharp and not keep him waiting there all night. The chaff and the humourous sallies to which he was subjected, and to which, of course, he had to provide prompt and effective reply, formed, indeed, his chief danger; for Toad was an animal with a strong sense of his own dignity, and the chaff was mostly (he thought) poor and clumsy, and the humour of the sallies entirely lacking. However, he kept his temper, though with great difficulty, suited his retorts to his company and his supposed character, and did his best not to overstep the limits of good taste.

It seemed hours before he crossed the last courtyard, rejected the pressing invitations from the last guardroom, and dodged the outspread arms of the last warder, pleading with simulated passion for just one farewell embrace. But at last he heard the wicket-gate in the great outer door click behind him, felt the fresh air of the outer world upon his anxious brow, and knew that he was free!

Dizzy with the easy success of his daring exploit, he walked quickly towards the lights of the town, not knowing in the least what he should do next, only quite certain of one thing, that he must remove himself as quickly as possible from the neighbourhood where the lady he was forced to represent was so well-known and so popular a character.

As he walked along, considering, his attention was caught by some red and green lights a little way off, to one side of the town, and the sound of the puffing and snorting of engines and the banging of shunted trucks fell on his ear. 'Aha!' he thought, 'this is a piece of luck! A railway station is the thing I want most in the whole world at this moment; and what's more, I needn't go through the town to get it, and shan't have to support this humiliating character by repartees which, though thoroughly effective, do not assist one's sense of self-respect.'

He made his way to the station accordingly, consulted a time-table, and found that a train, bound more or less in the direction of his home, was due to start in half-an-hour. 'More luck!' said Toad, his spirits rising rapidly, and went off to the booking-office to buy his ticket.

He gave the name of the station that he knew to be nearest to the village of which Toad Hall was the principal feature, and mechanically put his fingers, in search of the necessary money, where his waistcoat pocket should have been. But here the cotton gown, which had nobly stood by him so far, and which he had basely forgotten, intervened, and frustrated his efforts. In a sort of nightmare he struggled with the strange uncanny thing that seemed to hold his hands, turn all muscular strivings to water, and laugh at him all the time; while other travellers, forming up in a line behind, waited with impatience, making suggestions of more or less value and comments of more or less stringency and point. At last—somehow—he never rightly understood how—he burst the barriers, attained the goal, arrived at where all waistcoat pockets are eternally situated, and found—not only no money, but no pocket to hold it, and no waistcoat to hold the pocket!

To his horror he recollected that he had left both coat and waistcoat behind him in his cell, and with them his pocket-book, money, keys, watch, matches, pencil-case—all that makes life worth living, all that distinguished the many-pocketed animal, the lord of creation, from the inferior one-pocketed or no-pocketed productions that hop or trip about permissively, unequipped for the real contest.

In his misery he made one desperate effort to carry the thing off, and, with a return to his fine old manner—a blend of the Squire and the College Don—he said, 'Look here! I find I've left my purse behind. Just give me that ticket, will you, and I'll send the money on to-morrow? I'm well-known in these parts.'

The clerk stared at him and the rusty black bonnet a moment, and then laughed. 'I should think you were pretty well known in these parts,' he said, 'if you've tried this game on often. Here, stand away from the window, please, madam; you're obstructing the other passengers!'

An old gentleman who had been prodding him in the back for some moments here thrust him away, and, what was worse, addressed him as his good woman, which angered Toad more than anything that had occurred that evening.

Baffled and full of despair, he wandered blindly down the platform where the train was standing, and tears trickled down each side of his nose. It was hard, he thought, to be within sight of safety and almost of home, and to be baulked by the want of a few wretched shillings and by the pettifogging mistrustfulness of paid officials. Very soon his escape would be discovered, the hunt would be up, he would be caught, reviled, loaded with chains, dragged back again to prison, and bread-and-water and straw; his guards and penalties would be doubled; and O, what sarcastic remarks the girl would make! What was to be done? He was not swift of foot; his figure was unfortunately recognisable. Could he not squeeze under the seat of a carriage? He had seen this method adopted by schoolboys, when the journey-money provided by thoughtful parents had been diverted to other and better ends. As he pondered, he found himself opposite the engine, which was being oiled, wiped, and generally caressed by its affectionate driver, a burly man with an oil-can in one hand and a lump of cotton-waste in the other.

'Hullo, mother!' said the engine-driver, 'what's

the trouble? You don't look particularly cheerful.'

'O, sir!' said Toad, crying afresh, 'I am a poor unhappy washerwoman, and I've lost all my money, and can't pay for a ticket, and I *must* get home tonight somehow, and whatever I am to do I don't know. O dear, O dear!'

'That's a bad business, indeed,' said the engine-driver reflectively. 'Lost your money—and can't get home—and got some kids, too, waiting for you, I dare say?'

'Any amount of 'em,' sobbed Toad. 'And they'll be hungry—and playing with matches—and upsetting lamps, the little innocents!—and quarrelling, and going on generally. O dear, O dear!'

'Well, I'll tell you what I'll do,' said the good engine-driver. 'You're a washerwoman to your trade, says you. Very well, that's that. And I'm an engine-driver, as you well may see, and there's no denying it's terribly dirty work. Uses up a power of shirts, it does, till my missus is fair tired of washing of 'em. If you'll wash a few shirts for me when you get home, and send 'em along, I'll give you a ride on my engine. It's against the Company's regulations, but we're not so very particular in these out-of-the-way parts.'

The Toad's misery turned into rapture as he eagerly scrambled up into the cab of the engine. Of course, he had never washed a shirt in his life, and couldn't if he tried and, anyhow, he wasn't going to begin; but he thought: 'When I get safely home to Toad Hall, and have money again, and pockets to put it in, I will send the engine-driver enough to pay for quite a quantity of washing, and that will be the same thing, or better.'

The guard waved his welcome flag, the engine-driver whistled in cheerful response, and the train moved out of the station. As the speed increased, and the Toad could see on either side of him real fields, and trees, and hedges, and cows, and horses, all flying past him, and as he thought how every minute was bringing him nearer to Toad Hall, and sympathetic friends, and money to chink in his pocket, and a soft bed to sleep in, and good things to eat, and praise and admiration at the recital of his adventures and his surpassing cleverness, he began to skip up and down and shout and sing snatches of song, to the great astonishment of the engine-driver, who had come across washerwomen before, at long intervals, but never one at all like this.

They had covered many and many a mile, and Toad was already considering what he would have for supper as soon as he got home, when he noticed that the engine-driver, with a puzzled expression on his face, was leaning over the side of the engine and listening hard. Then he saw him climb on to the coals and gaze out over the top of the train; then he returned and said to Toad: 'It's very strange: we're the last train running in this direction to-night, yet I could be sworn that I heard another following us!'

Toad ceased his frivolous antics at once. He became grave and depressed, and a dull pain in the lower part of his spine, communicating itself to his legs, made him want to sit down and try desperately not to think of all the possibilities.

By this time the moon was shining brightly, and the engine-driver, steadying himself on the coal, could command a view of the line behind them for a long distance.

Presently he called out, 'I can see it clearly now! It is an engine, on our rails, coming along at a great pace! It looks as if we were being pursued!'

The miserable Toad, crouching in the coal-dust, tried hard to think of something to do, with dismal want of success.

'They are gaining on us fast!' cried the engine-driver. 'And the engine is crowded with the queerest lot of people! Men like ancient warders, waving halberds; policemen in their helmets, waving truncheons; and shabbily dressed men in pot-hats, obvious and unmistakable plain-clothes detectives even at this distance, waving revolvers and walking-sticks; all waving, and all shouting the same thing—"Stop, stop, stop!" '

Then Toad fell on his knees among the coals and, raising his clasped paws in supplication, cried, 'Save me, only save me, dear kind Mr. Engine-driver, and I will confess everything! I am not the simple washerwoman I seem to be! I have no children waiting for me, innocent or otherwise! I am a toad—the well-known and popular Mr. Toad, a landed proprietor; I have just escaped, by my great daring and cleverness, from a loathesome dungeon into which my enemies had flung me; and if those fellows on that engine recapture me, it will be chains and bread-and-water and straw and misery once more for poor, unhappy, innocent Toad!'

The engine-driver looked down upon him very sternly, and said, 'Now tell the truth; what were you put in prison for?'

'It was nothing very much,' said poor Toad, colouring deeply. 'I only borrowed a motor-car while the owners were at lunch; they had no need of it at the time. I didn't mean to steal it, really; but people—especially magistrates—take such harsh views of thoughtless and high-spirited actions.'

The engine-driver looked very grave and said, 'I fear that you have been indeed a wicked toad, and by rights I ought to give you up to offended justice. But you are evidently in sore trouble and distress, so I will not desert you. I don't hold with motor-cars, for one thing; and I don't hold with being ordered about by policemen when I'm on my own engine, for another. And the sight of an animal in tears always makes me feel queer and soft-hearted. So cheer up, Toad! I'll do my best, and we may beat them yet!'

They piled on more coals, shovelling furiously; the furnace roared, the sparks flew, the engine leapt and swung, but still their pursuers slowly gained. The engine-driver, with a sigh, wiped his brow with a handful of cotton-waste, and said, 'I'm afraid it's no good, Toad. You see, they are running light, and they have the better engine. There's just one thing left for us to do, and it's your only chance, so attend very carefully to what I tell you. A short way ahead of us is a long tunnel, and on the other side of that the line passes through a thick wood. Now, I will put on all the speed I can while we are running through the tunnel, but the other fellows will slow down a bit, naturally, for fear of an accident. When we are through, I will shut off steam and put on brakes as hard as I can, and the moment it's safe to do so you must jump and hide in the wood, before they get through the tunnel and see you. Then I will go full speed ahead again, and they can chase me if they like, for as long as they like, and as far as they like. Now mind and be ready to jump when I tell you!'

They piled on more coals, and the train shot into the tunnel, and the engine rushed and roared and rattled, till at last they shot out at the other end into fresh air and the peaceful moonlight, and saw the wood lying dark and helpful upon either side of the line. The driver shut off steam and put on brakes, the Toad got down on the step, and as the train slowed down to almost a walking pace he heard the driver call out, 'Now, jump!'

Toad jumped, rolled down a short embankment, picked himself up unhurt, scrambled into the wood and hid.

Peeping out, he saw his train get up speed again and disappear at a great pace. Then out of the tunnel burst the pursuing engine, roaring and whistling, her motley crew waving their various weapons and shouting, 'Stop! stop! stop!' When they were past, the Toad had a hearty laugh—for the first time since he was thrown into prison.

But he soon stopped laughing when he came to consider that it was now very late and dark and cold, and he was in an unknown wood, with no money and no chance of supper, and still far from friends and home; and the dead silence of everything, after the roar and rattle of the train, was something of a shock. He dared not leave the shelter of the trees, so he struck into the wood, with the idea of leaving the railway as far as possible behind him.

After so many weeks within walls, he found the wood strange and unfriendly and inclined, he thought, to make fun of him. Night-jars, sounding their mechanical rattle, made him think that the wood was full of searching warders, closing in on him. An owl, swooping noiselessly towards him, brushed his shoulder with its wing, making him jump with the horrid certainty that it was a hand; then flitted off, moth-like, laughing its low ho! ho! ho! which Toad thought in very poor taste. Once he met a fox, who stopped, looked him up and down in a sarcastic sort of way, and said, 'Hullo, washerwoman! Half a pair of socks and a pillow-case short this week! Mind it doesn't occur again!' and swaggered off, sniggering. Toad looked about for a stone to throw at him, but could not succeed in finding one, which vexed him more than anything. At last, cold, hungry, and tired out, he sought the shelter of a hollow tree, where with branches and dead leaves he made himself as comfortable a bed as he could, and slept soundly till the morning.

THE FURTHER ADVENTURES OF TOAD

* * *

As HE tramped along gaily, he thought of his adventures and escapes, and how when things seemed at their worst he had always managed to find a way out; and his pride and conceit began to swell within him. 'Ho, ho!' he said to himself as he marched along with his chin in the air, 'what a clever Toad I am! There is surely no animal equal to me for cleverness in the whole world! My enemies shut me up in prison, encircled by sentries, watched night and day by warders; I walk out through them all, by sheer ability coupled with courage. They pursue me with engines, and policemen, and revolvers; I snap my fingers at them, and vanish, laughing, into space. I am, unfortunately, thrown into a canal by a woman fat of body and very evil-minded. What of it? I swim ashore, I seize her horse, I ride off in triumph, and I sell the horse for a whole pocketful of money and an excellent breakfast! Ho, ho! I am

The Toad, the handsome, the popular, the successful Toad!' He got so puffed up with conceit that he made up a song as he walked in praise of himself, and sang it at the top of his voice, though there was no one to hear it but him. It was perhaps the most conceited song that any animal ever composed.

'The world has held great Heroes,
  As history-books have showed;
But never a name to go down to fame
  Compared with that of Toad!

'The clever men at Oxford
  Know all that there is to be knowed.
But they none of them know one half as much
  As intelligent Mr. Toad!

'The animals sat in the Ark and cried,
  Their tears in torrents flowed.
Who was it said, "There's land ahead?"
  Encouraging Mr. Toad!

'The army all saluted
  As they marched along the road.
Was it the King? Or Kitchener?
  No. It was Mr. Toad.

'The Queen and her Ladies-in-waiting
  Sat at the window and sewed.
She cried, "Look! who's that *handsome* man?"
  They answered, "Mr. Toad." '

There was a great deal more of the same sort, but too dreadfully conceited to be written down. These are some of the milder verses.

He sang as he walked, and he walked as he sang, and got more inflated every minute. But his pride was shortly to have a severe fall.

After some miles of country lanes he reached the high road, and as he turned into it and glanced along its white length, he saw approaching him a speck that turned into a dot and then into a blob, and then into something very familiar; and a double note of warning, only too well known, fell on his delighted ear.

'This is something like!' said the excited Toad. 'This is real life again, this is once more the great world from which I have been missed so long! I will hail them, my brothers of the wheel, and pitch them a yarn, of the sort that has been so successful hitherto; and they will give me a lift, of course, and then I will talk to them some more; and, perhaps, with luck, it may even end in my driving up to Toad Hall in a motor-car! That will be one in the eye for Badger!'

He stepped confidently out into the road to hail the motor-car, which came along at an easy pace, slowing down as it neared the lane; when suddenly he became very pale, his heart turned to water, his knees shook and yielded under him, and he doubled up and collapsed with a sickening pain in his interior. And well he might, the unhappy animal; for the approaching car was the very one he had stolen out of the yard of the Red Lion Hotel on that fatal day when all his troubles began! And the people in it were the very same people he had sat and watched at luncheon in the coffee-room!

He sank down in a shabby, miserable heap in the road, murmuring to himself in his despair, 'It's all up! It's all over now! Chains and policemen again! Prison again! Dry bread and water again! O, what a fool I have been! What did I want to go strutting about the country for, singing conceited songs, and hailing people in broad day on the high road, instead of hiding till nightfall and slipping home quietly by back ways! O hapless Toad! O ill-fated animal!'

The terrible motor-car drew slowly nearer and nearer, till at last he heard it stop just short of him. Two gentlemen got out and walked round the trembling heap of crumpled misery lying in the road, and one of them said, 'O dear! this is very sad! Here is a poor old thing—a washerwoman apparently—who has fainted in the road! Perhaps she is overcome by the heat, poor creature; or possibly she has not had any food to-day. Let us lift her into the car and take her to the nearest village, where doubtless she has friends.'

They tenderly lifted Toad into the motor-car and propped him up with soft cushions, and proceeded on their way.

When Toad heard them talk in so kind and sympathetic a way, and knew that he was not recognised, his courage began to revive, and he cautiously opened first one eye and then the other.

'Look!' said one of the gentlemen, 'she is better already. The fresh air is doing her good. How do you feel now, ma'am?'

'Thank you kindly, Sir,' said Toad in a feeble voice, 'I'm feeling a great deal better!' 'That's right,' said the gentleman. 'Now keep quite still, and, above all, don't try to talk.'

'I won't,' said Toad. 'I was only thinking, if I might sit on the front seat there, beside the driver, where I could get the fresh air full in my face, I should soon be all right again.'

'What a very sensible woman!' said the gentleman. 'Of course you shall.' So they carefully helped Toad into the front seat beside the driver, and on they went again.

Toad was almost himself again by now. He sat up, looked about him, and tried to beat down the tremors, the yearnings, the old cravings that rose up and beset him and took possession of him entirely.

'It is fate!' he said to himself. 'Why strive? why struggle?' and he turned to the driver at his side.

'Please, Sir,' he said, 'I wish you would kindly let me try and drive the car for a little. I've been watching you carefully, and it looks so easy and so interesting, and I should like to be able to tell my friends that once I had driven a motor-car!'

The driver laughed at the proposal, so heartily that the gentleman inquired what the matter was. When he heard, he said, to Toad's delight, 'Bravo, ma'am! I like your spirit. Let her have a try, and look after her. She won't do any harm.'

Toad eagerly scrambled into the seat vacated by the driver, took the steering-wheel in his hands, listened with affected humility to the instructions given him, and set the car in motion, but very slowly and carefully at first, for he was determined to be prudent.

The gentlemen behind clapped their hands and applauded, and Toad heard them saying, 'How well she does it! Fancy a washerwoman driving a car as well as that, the first time!'

Toad went a little faster; then faster still, and faster.

He heard the gentlemen call out warningly, 'Be careful, washerwoman!' And this annoyed him, and he began to lose his head.

The driver tried to interfere, but he pinned him down in his seat with one elbow, and put on full speed. The rush of air in his face, the hum of the engines, and the light jump of the car beneath him intoxicated his weak brain. 'Washerwoman indeed!' he shouted recklessly. 'Ho! ho! I am the Toad, the motor-car snatcher, the prison-breaker, the Toad who always escapes! Sit still, and you shall know what driving really is, for you are in the hands of the famous, the skilful, the entirely fearless Toad!'

With a cry of horror the whole party rose and flung themselves on him. 'Seize him!' they cried, 'seize the Toad, the wicked animal who stole our motor-car! Bind him, chain him, drag him to the nearest police-station! Down with the desperate and dangerous Toad!'

Alas! they should have thought, they ought to have been more prudent, they should have remembered to stop the motor-car somehow before playing any pranks of that sort. With a half-turn of the wheel the Toad sent the car crashing through the low hedge that ran along the roadside. One mighty bound, a violent shock, and the wheels of the car were churning up the thick mud of a horse-pond.

Toad found himself flying through the air with the strong upward rush and delicate curve of a swallow. He liked the motion, and was just beginning to wonder whether it would go on until he developed wings and turned into a Toad-bird, when he landed on his back with a thump, in the soft rich grass of a meadow. Sitting up, he could just see the motor-car in the pond, nearly submerged; the gentlemen and the driver, encumbered by their long coats, were floundering helplessly in the water.

He picked himself up rapidly, and set off running across country as hard as he could, scrambling through hedges, jumping ditches, pounding across fields, till he was breathless and weary, and had to settle down into an easy walk. When he had recovered his breath somewhat, and was able to think calmly, he began to giggle, and from giggling he took to laughing, and he laughed till he had to sit down under a hedge. 'Ho, ho!' he cried, in ecstasies of self-admiration, 'Toad again! Toad, as usual, comes out on top! Who was it got them to give him a lift? Who managed to get on the front seat for the sake of fresh air? Who persuaded them into letting him see if he could drive? Who landed them all in a horse-pond? Who escaped, flying gaily and unscathed through the air, leaving the narrow-minded, grudging, timid excursionists in the mud where they should rightly be? Why, Toad, of course; clever Toad, great Toad, *good* Toad!'

Then he burst into song again, and chanted with uplifted voice—

'The motor-car went Poop-poop-poop,
  As it raced along the road.
Who was it steered it into a pond?
  Ingenious Mr. Toad!

O, how clever I am! How clever, how clever, how very clev——'

A slight noise at a distance behind him made him turn his head and look. O horror! O misery! O despair!

About two fields off, a chauffeur in his leather gaiters and two large rural policemen were visible, running towards him as hard as they could go!

Poor Toad sprang to his feet and pelted away again, his heart in his mouth. 'O, my!' he gasped, as he panted along, 'what an *ass* I am! What a *con-*

ceited and heedless ass! Swaggering again! Shouting and singing songs again! Sitting still and gassing again! O my! O my! O my!'

He glanced back, and saw to his dismay that they were gaining on him. On he ran desperately, but kept looking back, and saw that they still gained steadily. He did his best, but he was a fat animal, and his legs were short, and still they gained. He could hear them close behind him now. Ceasing to heed where he was going, he struggled on blindly and wildly, looking back over his shoulder at the now triumphant enemy, when suddenly the earth failed under his feet, he grasped at the air, and, splash! he found himself head over ears in deep water, rapid water, water that bore him along with a force he could not contend with; and he knew that in his blind panic he had run straight into the river!

He rose to the surface and tried to grasp the reeds and the rushes that grew along the water's edge close under the bank, but the stream was so strong that it tore them out of his hands. 'O my!' gasped poor Toad, 'if ever I steal a motor-car again! If ever I sing another conceited song'—then down he went, and came up breathless and spluttering. Presently he saw that he was approaching a big dark hole in the bank, just above his head, and as the stream bore him past he reached up with a paw and caught hold of the edge and held on. Then slowly and with difficulty he drew himself up out of the water, till at last he was able to rest his elbows on the edge of the hole. There he remained for some minutes, puffing and panting, for he was quite exhausted.

As he sighed and blew and stared before him into the dark hole, some bright small thing shone and twinkled in its depths, moving towards him. As it approached, a face grew up gradually around it, and it was a familiar face!

Brown and small, with whiskers.

Grave and round, with neat ears and silky hair.

It was the Water Rat.

THE RAT put out a neat little brown paw, gripped Toad firmly by the scruff of the neck, and gave a great hoist and a pull; and the water-logged Toad came up slowly but surely over the edge of the hole, till at last he stood safe and sound in the hall, streaked with mud and weed to be sure, and with the water streaming off him, but happy and high-spirited as of old, now that he found himself once more in the house of a friend, and dodgings and evasions were over, and he could lay aside a disguise that was unworthy of his position and wanted such a lot of living up to.

'O, Ratty!' he cried. 'I've been through such times since I saw you last, you can't think! Such trials, such sufferings, and all so nobly borne! Then such escapes, such disguises, such subterfuges, and all so cleverly planned and carried out: Been in prison—got out of it, of course! Been thrown into a canal—swam ashore! Stole a horse—sold him for a large sum of money! Humbugged everybody—made 'em all do exactly what I wanted! Oh, I *am* a smart Toad, and no mistake! What do you think my last exploit was? Just hold on till I tell you——'

'Toad,' said the Water Rat, gravely and firmly, 'you go off upstairs at once, and take off that old cotton rag that looks as if it might formerly have belonged to some washerwoman, and clean yourself thoroughly, and put on some of my clothes, and try and come down looking like a gentleman if you *can;* for a more shabby, bedraggled, disreputable-looking object than you are I never set eyes on in my whole life! Now, stop swaggering and arguing, and be off! I'll have something to say to you later!'

Toad was at first inclined to stop and do some talking back at him. He had had enough of being ordered about when he was in prison, and here was the thing being begun all over again, apparently; and by a Rat, too! However, he caught sight of himself in the looking-glass over the hat-stand, with the rusty black bonnet perched rakishly over one eye, and he changed his mind and went very quickly and humbly upstairs to the Rat's dressing-room. There he had a thorough wash and brush-up, changed his clothes, and stood for a long time before the glass, contemplating himself with pride and pleasure, and thinking what utter idiots all the people must have been to have ever mistaken him for one moment for a washerwoman.

By the time he came down again luncheon was on the table, and very glad Toad was to see it, for he had been through some trying experiences and had taken much hard exercise since the excellent breakfast provided for him by the gipsy. While they ate Toad told the Rat all his adventures, dwelling chiefly on his own cleverness, and presence of mind in emergencies, and cunning in tight places; and rather making out that he had been having a gay and highly-coloured experience. But the more he talked and boasted, the more grave and silent the Rat became.

When at last Toad had talked himself to a standstill, there was silence for a while; and then the Rat said, 'Now, Toady, I don't want to give you pain, after all you've been through already; but, seriously, don't you see what an awful ass you've been making of yourself? On your own admission you have been handcuffed, imprisoned, starved, chased, terrified out of your life, insulted, jeered at, and ignominiously flung into the water—by a woman, too! Where's the amusement in that? Where does the fun come in? And all because you must needs go and steal a motor-car. You know that you've never had anything but trouble from motor-cars from the moment you first set eyes on one. But if you *will* be mixed up with them—as you generally are, five minutes after you've started—why *steal* them? Be a cripple, if you think it's exciting; be a bankrupt, for a change, if you've set your mind on it: but why choose to be a convict? When are you going to be sensible, and think of your friends, and try and be a credit to them? Do you suppose it's any pleasure to me, for instance, to hear animals saying, as I go about, that I'm the chap that keeps company with gaol-birds?'

Now, it was a very comforting point in Toad's character that he was a thoroughly good-hearted animal, and never minded being jawed by those who were his real friends. And even when most set upon a thing, he was always able to see the other side of the question. So although, while the Rat was talking so seriously, he kept saying to himself mutinously, 'But it *was* fun, though! Awful fun!' and making strange suppressed noises inside him, k-i-ck-ck-ck, and poop-p-p, and other sounds resembling stifled snorts, or the opening of soda-water bottles, yet when the Rat had quite finished, he heaved a deep sigh and said, very nicely and humbly, 'Quite right, Ratty! How *sound* you always are! Yes, I've been a conceited old ass, I can quite see that; but now I'm going to be a good Toad, and not do it any more. As for motor-cars, I've not been at all so keen about them since my last ducking in that river of yours. The fact is, while I was hanging on to the edge of your hole and getting my breath, I had a sudden idea—a really brilliant idea—connected with motor-boats—there, there! don't take on so, old chap, and stamp, and upset things; it was only an idea, and we won't talk any more about it now. We'll have our coffee, *and* a smoke, and a quiet chat, and then I'm going to stroll quietly down to Toad Hall, and get into clothes of my own, and set things going again on the old lines. I've had enough of adventures. I shall lead a quiet, steady, respectable life, pottering about my property, and improving it, and doing a little landscape gardening at times. There will always be a bit of dinner for my friends when they come to see me; and I shall keep a pony-chaise to jog about the country in, just as I used to in the good old days, before I got restless, and wanted to *do* things.'

'Stroll quietly down to Toad Hall?' cried the Rat, greatly excited. 'What are you talking about? Do you mean to say you haven't *heard?*'

'Heard what?' said Toad, turning rather pale. 'Go on, Ratty! Quick! Don't spare me! What haven't I heard?'

'Do you mean to tell me,' shouted the Rat, thumping with his little fist upon the table, 'that you've heard nothing about the Stoats and Weasels?'

'What, the Wild Wooders?' cried Toad, trembling in every limb. 'No, not a word! What have they been doing?'

'—And how they've been and taken Toad Hall?' continued the Rat.

Toad leaned his elbows on the table, and his chin on his paws; and a large tear welled up in each of his eyes, overflowed and splashed on the table, plop! plop!

'Go on, Ratty,' he murmured presently; 'tell me all. The worst is over. I am an animal again. I can bear it.'

'When you—got—into that—that—trouble of yours,' said the Rat, slowly and impressively; 'I mean, when you—disappeared from society for a time, over that misunderstanding about a—a machine, you know—'

Toad merely nodded.

'Well, it was a good deal talked about down here, naturally,' continued the Rat, 'not only along the river-side, but even in the Wild Wood. Animals took sides, as always happens. The River-bankers stuck up for you, and said you had been infamously treated, and there was no justice to be had in the land nowadays. But the Wild Wood animals said hard things, and served you right, and it was time this sort of thing was stopped. And they got very cocky, and went about saying you were done for this time! You would never come back again, never, never!'

Toad nodded once more, keeping silence.

'That's the sort of little beasts they are,' the Rat went on. 'But Mole and Badger, they stuck out, through thick and thin, that you would come back again soon, somehow. They didn't know exactly how, but somehow!'

Toad began to sit up in his chair again, and to smirk a little.

'They argued from history,' continued the Rat. 'They said that no criminal laws had ever been known to prevail against cheek and plausibility such as yours, combined with the power of a long purse. So they arranged to move their things in to Toad Hall, and sleep there, and keep it aired, and have it all ready for you when you turned up. They didn't guess what was going to happen, of course; still, they had their suspicions of the Wild Wood animals. Now I come to the most painful and tragic part of my story. One dark night—it was a *very* dark night, and blowing hard, too, and raining simply cats and dogs—a band of weasels, armed to the teeth, crept silently up the carriage-drive to the front entrance. Simultaneously, a body of desperate ferrets, advancing through the kitchen-garden, possessed themselves of the backyard and offices; while a company of skirmishing stoats who stuck at nothing occupied the conservatory and the billiard-room, and held the French windows opening on to the lawn.

'The Mole and the Badger were sitting by the fire in the smoking-room, telling stories and suspecting nothing, for it wasn't a night for any animals to be out in, when those bloodthirsty villains broke down the doors and rushed in upon them from every side. They made the best fight they could, but what was the good? They were unarmed, and taken by surprise, and what can two animals do against hundreds? They took and beat them severely with sticks, those two poor faithful creatures, and turned them out into the cold and the wet, with many insulting and uncalled-for remarks!'

Here the unfeeling Toad broke into a snigger, and then pulled himself together and tried to look particularly solemn.

'And the Wild Wooders have been living in Toad Hall ever since,' continued the Rat; 'and going on simply anyhow! Lying in bed half the day, and breakfast at all hours, and the place in such a mess

(I'm told) it's not fit to be seen! Eating your grub, and drinking your drink, and making bad jokes about you, and singing vulgar songs, about—well, about prisons and magistrates, and policemen; horrid personal songs, with no humour in them. And they're telling the tradespeople and everybody that they've come to stay for good.'

'Oh, have they!' said Toad, getting up and seizing a stick. 'I'll jolly soon see about that!'

'It's no good, Toad!' called the Rat after him. 'You'd better come back and sit down; you'll only get into trouble.'

But the Toad was off, and there was no holding him. He marched rapidly down the road, his stick over his shoulder, fuming and muttering to himself in his anger, till he got near his front gate, when suddenly there popped up from behind the palings a long yellow ferret with a gun.

'Who comes there?' said the ferret sharply.

'Stuff and nonsense!' said Toad, very angrily. 'What do you mean by talking like that to me? Come out of that at once, or I'll——'

The ferret said never a word, but he brought his gun up to his shoulder. Toad prudently dropped flat in the road, and *Bang!* a bullet whistled over his head.

The startled Toad scrambled to his feet and

scampered off down the road as hard as he could; and as he ran he heard the ferret laughing and other horrid thin little laughs taking it up and carrying on the sound.

He went back, very crestfallen, and told the Water Rat.

'What did I tell you?' said the Rat. 'It's no good. They've got sentries posted, and they are all armed. You must just wait.'

Still, Toad was not inclined to give in all at once. So he got out the boat, and set off rowing up the river to where the garden front of Toad Hall came down to the waterside.

Arriving within sight of his old home, he rested on his oars and surveyed the land cautiously. All seemed very peaceful and deserted and quiet. He could see the whole front of Toad Hall, glowing in the evening sunshine, the pigeons settling by twos and threes along the straight line of the roof; the garden, a blaze of flowers; the creek that led up to the boat-house, the little wooden bridge that crossed it; all tranquil, uninhabited, apparently waiting for his return. He would try the boat-house first, he thought. Very warily he paddled up to the mouth of the creek, and was just passing under the bridge, when . . . *Crash!*

A great stone, dropped from above, smashed

through the bottom of the boat. It filled and sank, and Toad found himself struggling in deep water. Looking up, he saw two stoats leaning over the parapet of the bridge and watching him with great glee. 'It will be your head next time, Toady!' they called out to him. The indignant Toad swam to shore, while the stoats laughed and laughed, supporting each other, and laughed again, till they nearly had two fits—that is, one fit each, of course.

The Toad retraced his weary way on foot, and related his disappointing experiences to the Water Rat once more.

'Well, *what* did I tell you?' said the Rat very crossly. 'And, now, look here! See what you've been and done! Lost me my boat that I was so fond of, that's what you've done! And simply ruined that nice suit of clothes that I lent you! Really, Toad, of all the trying animals—I wonder you manage to keep any friends at all!'

The Toad saw at once how wrongly and foolishly he had acted. He admitted his errors and wrongheadedness and made a full apology to Rat for losing his boat and spoiling his clothes. And he wound up by saying, with that frank self-surrender which always disarmed his friends' criticism and won them back to his side, 'Ratty! I see that I have been a headstrong and a wilful Toad! Henceforth, believe me, I will be humble and submissive, and will take no action without your kind advice and full approval!'

'If that is really so,' said the good-natured Rat, already appeased, 'then my advice to you is, considering the lateness of the hour, to sit down and have your supper, which will be on the table in a minute, and be very patient. For I am convinced that we can do nothing until we have seen the Mole and the Badger, and heard their latest news, and held conference and taken their advice in this difficult matter.'

'Oh, ah, yes, of course, the Mole and the Badger,' said Toad, lightly. 'What's become of them, the dear fellows? I had forgotten all about them.'

'Well may you ask!' said the Rat reproachfully. 'While you were riding about the country in expensive motor-cars, and galloping proudly on blood-horses, and breakfasting on the fat of the land, those two poor devoted animals have been camping out in the open, in every sort of weather, living very rough by day and lying very hard by night; watching over your house, patrolling your boundaries, keeping a constant eye on the stoats and the weasels, scheming and planning and contriving how to get your property back for you. You don't deserve to have such true and loyal friends, Toad, you don't, really. Some day, when it's too late, you'll be sorry you didn't value them more while you had them!'

'I'm an ungrateful beast, I know,' sobbed Toad, shedding bitter tears. 'Let me go out and find them, out into the cold, dark night, and share their hardships, and try and prove by——Hold on a bit! Surely I heard the chink of dishes on a tray! Supper's here at last, hooray! Come on, Ratty!'

The Rat remembered that poor Toad had been on prison fare for a considerable time, and that large allowances had therefore to be made. He followed him to the table accordingly, and hospitably encouraged him in his gallant efforts to make up for past privations.

They had just finished their meal and resumed their arm-chairs, when there came a heavy knock at the door.

Toad was nervous, but the Rat, nodding mysteriously at him, went straight up to the door and opened it, and in walked Mr. Badger.

He had all the appearance of one who for some nights had been kept away from home and all its little comforts and conveniences. His shoes were covered with mud, and he was looking very rough and touzled; but then he had never been a very smart man, the Badger, at the best of times. He came solemnly up to Toad, shook him by the paw, and said, 'Welcome home, Toad! Alas! what am I saying? Home, indeed! This is a poor home-coming. Unhappy Toad!' Then he turned his back on him, sat down to the table, drew his chair up, and helped himself to a large slice of cold pie.

Toad was quite alarmed at this very serious and portentous style of greeting; but the Rat whispered to him, 'Never mind; don't take any notice; and don't say anything to him just yet. He's always rather low and despondent when he's wanting his victuals. In half an hour's time he'll be quite a different animal.'

So they waited in silence, and presently there came another and a lighter knock. The Rat, with a nod to Toad, went to the door and ushered in the Mole, very shabby and unwashed, with bits of hay and straw sticking in his fur.

'Hooray! Here's old Toad!' cried the Mole, his face beaming. 'Fancy having you back again!' And he began to dance round him. 'We never dreamt you would turn up so soon! Why, you must have managed to escape, you clever, ingenious, intelligent Toad!'

The Rat, alarmed, pulled him by the elbow; but it was too late. Toad was puffing and swelling already.

'Clever? O, no!' he said. 'I'm not really clever,

according to my friends. I've only broken out of the strongest prison in England, that's all! And captured a railway train and escaped on it, that's all! And disguised myself and gone about the country humbugging everybody, that's all! O, no! I'm a stupid ass, I am! I'll tell you one or two of my little adventures, Mole, and you shall judge for yourself!'

'Well, well,' said the Mole, moving towards the supper-table; 'supposing you talk while I eat. Not a bite since breakfast! O my! O my!' And he sat down and helped himself liberally to cold beef and pickles.

Toad straddled on the hearth-rug, thrust his paw into his trouser-pocket and pulled out a handful of silver. 'Look at that!' he cried, displaying it. 'That's not so bad, is it, for a few minutes' work? And how do you think I done it, Mole? Horse-dealing! That's how I done it!'

'Go on, Toad,' said the Mole, immensely interested.

'Toad, do be quiet, please!' said the Rat. 'And don't you egg him on, Mole, when you know what he is; but please tell us as soon as possible what the position is, and what's best to be done, now that Toad is back at last.'

'The position's about as bad as it can be,' replied the Mole grumpily; 'and as for what's to be done, why, blest if I know! The Badger and I have been round and round the place, by night and by day; always the same thing. Sentries posted everywhere, guns poked out at us, stones thrown at us; always an animal on the look-out, and when they see us, my! how they do laugh! That's what annoys me most!'

'It's a very difficult situation,' said the Rat, reflecting deeply. 'But I think I see now, in the depths of my mind, what Toad really ought to do. I will tell you. He ought to——'

'No, he oughtn't!' shouted the Mole, with his mouth full. 'Nothing of the sort! You don't understand. What he ought to do is, he ought to——'

'Well, I shan't do it, anyway!' cried Toad, getting excited. 'I'm not going to be ordered about by you fellows! It's my house we're talking about, and I know exactly what to do, and I'll tell you. I'm going to——'

By this time they were all three talking at once, at the top of their voices, and the noise was simply deafening, when a thin, dry voice made itself heard, saying, 'Be quiet at once, all of you!' and instantly every one was silent.

It was the Badger, who, having finished his pie, had turned round in his chair and was looking at them severely. When he saw that he had secured their attention, and that they were evidently waiting for him to address them, he turned back to the table again and reached out for the cheese. And so great was the respect commanded by the solid qualities of that admirable animal, that not another word was uttered until he had quite finished his repast and brushed the crumbs from his knees. The Toad fidgeted a good deal, but the Rat held him firmly down.

When the Badger had quite done, he got up from his seat and stood before the fireplace, reflecting deeply. At last he spoke.

'Toad!' he said severely. 'You bad, troublesome little animal! Aren't you ashamed of yourself? What do you think your father, my old friend, would have said if he had been here to-night, and had known of all your goings on?'

Toad, who was on the sofa by this time, with his legs up, rolled over on his face, shaken by sobs of contrition.

'There, there!' went on the Badger, more kindly. 'Never mind. Stop crying. We're going to let bygones be bygones, and try and turn over a new leaf. But what the Mole says is quite true. The stoats are on guard, at every point, and they make the best sentinels in the world. It's quite useless to think of attacking the place. They're too strong for us.'

'Then it's all over,' sobbed the Toad, crying into the sofa cushions. 'I shall go and enlist for a soldier, and never see my dear Toad Hall any more!'

'Come, cheer up, Toady!' said the Badger. 'There are more ways of getting back a place than taking it by storm. I haven't said my last word yet. Now I'm going to tell you a great secret.'

Toad sat up slowly and dried his eyes. Secrets had an immense attraction for him, because he never could keep one, and he enjoyed the sort of unhallowed thrill he experienced when he went and told another animal, after having faithfully promised not to.

'There—is—an—underground—passage,' said the Badger, impressively, 'that leads from the river-bank, quite near here, right up into the middle of Toad Hall.'

'O, nonsense! Badger,' said Toad, rather airily. 'You've been listening to some of the yarns they spin in the public-houses about here. I know every inch of Toad Hall, inside and out. Nothing of the sort, I do assure you!'

'My young friend,' said the Badger, with great severity, 'your father, who was a worthy animal—a lot worthier than some others I know—was a particular friend of mine, and told me a great deal he wouldn't have dreamt of telling you. He discovered that passage—he didn't make it, of course; that was done hundreds of years before he ever came to live there—and he repaired it and cleaned it out, because he thought it might come in useful some day, in case of trouble or danger; and he showed it to me. "Don't let my son know about it," he said. "He's a good boy, but very light and volatile in character, and simply cannot hold his tongue. If he's ever in a real fix, and it would be of use to him, you may tell him about the secret passage; but not before." '

The other animals looked hard at Toad to see how he would take it. Toad was inclined to be sulky at first; but he brightened up immediately, like the good fellow he was.

'Well, well,' he said; 'perhaps I am a bit of a talker. A popular fellow such as I am—my friends get round me—we chaff, we sparkle, we tell witty stories—and somehow my tongue gets wagging. I have the gift of conversation. I've been told I ought to have a *salon*, whatever that may be. Never mind. Go on, Badger. How's this passage of yours going to help us?'

'I've found out a thing or two lately,' continued the Badger. 'I got Otter to disguise himself as a sweep and call at the back-door with brushes over his shoulder, asking for a job. There's going to be a big banquet to-morrow night. It's somebody's birthday—the Chief Weasel's, I believe—and all the weasels will be gathered together in the dining hall, eating and drinking and laughing and carrying on, suspecting nothing. No guns, no swords, no sticks, no arms of any sort whatever!'

'But the sentinels will be posted as usual,' remarked the Rat.

'Exactly,' said the Badger; 'that is my point. The weasels will trust entirely to their excellent sentinels. And that is where the passage comes in. That very useful tunnel leads right up under the butler's pantry, next to the dining-hall!'

'Aha! that squeaky board in the butler's pantry!' said Toad. 'Now I understand it!'

'We shall creep out quietly into the butler's pantry—' cried the Mole.

'—with our pistols and swords and sticks—' shouted the Rat.

'—and rush in upon them,' said the Badger.

'—and whack 'em, and whack 'em, and whack 'em!' cried the Toad in ecstasy, running round and round the room, and jumping over the chairs.

'Very well, then,' said the Badger, resuming his usual dry manner, 'our plan is settled, and there's nothing more for you to argue and squabble about. So, as it's getting very late, all of you go right off to bed at once. We will make all the necessary arrangements in the course of the morning to-morrow.'

WHEN IT BEGAN TO GROW DARK, the Rat, with an air of excitement and mystery, summoned them back into the parlour, stood each of them up alongside of his little heap, and proceeded to dress them up for the coming expedition. He was very earnest and thorough-going about it, and the affair took quite a long time. First, there was a belt to go round each animal, and then a sword to be stuck into each belt, and then a cutlass on the other side to balance it. Then a pair of pistols, a policeman's truncheon, several sets of handcuffs, some bandages and sticking-plaster, and a flask and a sandwich-case. The Badger laughed good-humouredly and said, 'All right, Ratty! It amuses you and it doesn't hurt me. I'm going to do all I've got to do with this here stick.' But the Rat only said, '*Please,* Badger. You know I shouldn't like you to blame me afterwards and say I had forgotten *anything!*'

When all was quite ready, the Badger took a dark lantern in one paw, grasped his great stick with the other, and said, 'Now then, follow me!

Mole first, 'cos I'm very pleased with him; Rat next; Toad last. And look here, Toady! Don't you chatter so much as usual, or you'll be sent back, as sure as fate!'

The Toad was so anxious not to be left out that he took up the inferior position assigned to him without a murmur, and the animals set off. The Badger led them along by the river for a little way, and then suddenly swung himself over the edge into a hole in the river-bank, a little above the water. The Mole and the Rat followed silently, swinging themselves successfully into the hole as they had seen the Badger do; but when it came to Toad's turn, of course he managed to slip and fall into the water with a loud splash and a squeal of alarm. He was hauled out by his friends, rubbed down and wrung out hastily, comforted and set on his legs; but the Badger was seriously angry, and told him that the very next time he made a fool of himself he would most certainly be left behind.

So at last they were in the secret passage, and the cutting-out expedition had really begun!

It was cold, and dark, and damp, and low, and narrow, and poor Toad began to shiver, partly from dread of what might be before him, partly because he was wet through. The lantern was far ahead, and he could not help lagging behind a little in the darkness. Then he heard the Rat call out warningly, '*Come* on Toad!' and a terror seized him of being left behind, alone in the darkness, and he 'came on' with such a rush that he upset the Rat into the Mole and the Mole into the Badger, and for a moment all was confusion. The Badger thought they were being attacked from behind, and, as there was no room to use a stick or a cutlass, drew a pistol, and was on the point of putting a bullet into Toad. When he found out what had really happened he was very angry indeed, and said, 'Now this time that tiresome Toad *shall* be left behind!'

But Toad whimpered, and the other two promised that they would be answerable for his good conduct, and at last the Badger was pacified, and the procession moved on; only this time the Rat brought up the rear, with a firm grip on the shoulder of Toad.

So they groped and shuffled along, with their ears pricked up and their paws on their pistols, till at last the Badger said, 'We ought by now to be pretty nearly under the Hall.'

Then suddenly they heard, far away as it might be, and yet apparently nearly over their heads, a confused murmur of sound, as if people were shouting and cheering and stamping on the floor and hammering on tables. The Toad's nervous terrors all returned, but the Badger only remarked placidly, 'They *are* doing it, the Weasels!'

The passage now began to slope upwards; they groped onward a little further, and then the noise broke out again, quite distinct this time, and very close above them. 'Ooo-ray-oo-ray-oo-ray-ooray!' they heard, and the stamping of little feet on the floor, and the clinking of glasses as little fists pounded on the table. '*What* a time they're having!' said the Badger. 'Come on!' They hurried along the passage till it came to a full stop, and they found themselves standing under the trap-door that led up into the butler's pantry.

Such a tremendous noise was going on in the banqueting-hall that there was little danger of their being overheard. The Badger said, 'Now, boys, all together!' and the four of them put their shoulders to the trap-door and heaved it back. Hoisting each other up, they found themselves standing in the pantry, with only a door between them and the banqueting-hall, where their unconscious enemies were carousing.

The noise, as they emerged from the passage, was simply deafening. At last, as the cheering and hammering slowly subsided, a voice could be made out saying, 'Well, I do not propose to detain you much longer'—(great applause)—'but before I resume my seat'—(renewed cheering)—'I should like to say one word about our kind host, Mr. Toad. We all know Toad!'—(great laughter)—'*Good* Toad, *modest* Toad, *honest* Toad!' (shrieks of merriment).

'Only just let me get at him!' muttered Toad, grinding his teeth.

'Hold hard a minute!' said the Badger, restraining him with difficulty. 'Get ready, all of you!'

'—Let me sing you a little song' went on the voice, 'which I have composed on the subject of Toad'—(prolonged applause).

Then the Chief Weasel—for it was he—began in a high, squeaky voice—

'Toad he went a-pleasuring
Gaily down the street—'

The Badger drew himself up, took a firm grip on his stick with both paws, glanced round at his comrades, and cried—

'The hour is come! Follow me!'

And flung the door open wide.

My!

What a squealing and a squeaking and a screeching filled the air!

Well might the terrified weasels dive under the

tables and spring madly up at the windows! Well might the ferrets rush wildly for the fireplace and get hopelessly jammed in the chimney! Well might tables and chairs be upset, and glass and china be sent crashing on the floor, in the panic of that terrible moment when the four Heroes strode wrathfully into the room! The mighty Badger, his whiskers bristling, his great cudgel whistling through the air; Mole, black and grim, brandishing his stick and shouting his awful war-cry, 'A Mole! A Mole!' Rat, desperate and determined, his belt bulging with weapons of every age and every variety; Toad, frenzied with excitement and injured pride, swollen to twice his ordinary size, leaping into the air and emitting Toad-whoops that chilled them to the marrow! 'Toad he went a-pleasuring!' he yelled. *'I'll* pleasure 'em!' and he went straight for the Chief Weasel. They were but four in all, but to the panic-stricken weasels the hall seemed full of monstrous animals, grey, black, brown and yellow, whooping and flourishing enormous cudgels; and they broke and fled with squeals of terror and dismay, this way and that, through the windows, up the chimney, anywhere to get out of reach of those terrible sticks.

The affair was soon over. Up and down, the whole length of the hall, strode the four Friends, whacking with their sticks at every head that showed itself; and in five minutes the room was cleared. Through the broken windows the shrieks of terrified weasels escaping across the lawn were borne faintly to their ears; on the floor lay prostrate some dozen or so of the enemy, on whom the Mole was busily engaged in fitting handcuffs. The Badger, resting from his labours, leant on his stick and wiped his honest brow.

'Mole,' he said, 'you're the best of fellows! Just cut along outside and look after those stoat-sentries of yours, and see what they're doing. I've an idea that, thanks to you, we shan't have much trouble from *them* to-night!'

The Mole vanished promptly through a window; and the Badger bade the other two set a table on its legs again, pick up knives and forks and plates and glasses from the *débris* on the floor, and see if they could find materials for a supper. 'I want some grub, I do,' he said, in that rather common way he had of speaking. 'Stir your stumps, Toad, and look lively! We've got your house back for you, and you don't offer us so much as a sandwich.'

Toad felt rather hurt that the Badger didn't say pleasant things to him, as he had to the Mole, and tell him what a fine fellow he was, and how splendidly he had fought; for he was rather particularly pleased with himself and the way he had gone for the Chief Weasel and sent him flying across the table with one blow of his stick. But he bustled about, and so did the Rat, and soon they found some guava jelly in a glass dish, and a cold chicken, a tongue that had hardly been touched, some trifle, and quite a lot of lobster salad; and in the pantry they came upon a basketful of French rolls and any quantity of cheese, butter, and celery. They were just about to sit down when the Mole clambered in through the window, chuckling, with an armful of rifles.

'It's all over,' he reported. 'From what I can make out, as soon as the stoats, who were very nervous and jumpy already, heard the shrieks and the yells and the uproar inside the hall, some of them threw down their rifles and fled. The others stood fast for a bit, but when the weasels came rushing out upon them they thought they were betrayed; and the stoats grappled with the weasels, and the weasels fought to get away, and they wrestled and wriggled and punched each other, and rolled over and over, till most of 'em rolled into the river! They've all disappeared by now, one way or another; and I've got their rifles. So *that's* all right!'

'Excellent and deserving animal!' said the Badger, his mouth full of chicken and trifle. 'Now, there's just one more thing I want you to do, Mole, before you sit down to your supper along of us; and I wouldn't trouble you only I know I can trust you to see a thing done, and I wish I could say the same of every one I know. I'd send Rat, if he wasn't a poet. I want you to take those fellows on the floor there upstairs with you, and have some bedrooms cleaned out and tidied up and made really comfortable. See that they sweep *under* the beds, and put clean sheets and pillow-cases on, and turn down one corner of the bed-clothes, just as you know it ought to be done; and have a can of hot water, and clean towels, and fresh cakes of soap, put in each room. And then you can give them a licking a-piece, if it's any satisfaction to you, and put them out by the back-door, and we shan't see any more of *them*, I fancy. And then come along and have some of this cold tongue. It's first rate. I'm very pleased with you, Mole!'

The goodnatured Mole picked up a stick, formed his prisoners up in a line on the floor, gave them the order 'Quick march!' and led his squad off to the upper floor. After a time, he appeared again, smiling, and said that every room was ready, and as clean as a new pin. 'And I didn't have to lick them, either,' he added. 'I thought, on the whole, they had had licking enough for one night, and the weasels, when I put the point to them, quite agreed with me, and said they wouldn't think of troubling me. They were very penitent, and said they were extremely sorry for what they had done, but it was all the fault of the Chief Weasel and the stoats, and if ever they could do anything for us at any time to make up, we had only got to mention it. So I gave them a roll a-piece, and let them out at the back, and off they ran, as hard as they could!'

Then the Mole pulled his chair up to the table, and pitched into the cold tongue; and Toad, like the gentleman he was, put all his jealousy from him, and said heartily, 'Thank you kindly, dear Mole, for all your pains and trouble to-night, and especially for your cleverness this morning!' The Badger was pleased at that, and said, 'There spoke my brave Toad!' So they finished their supper in great joy and contentment, and presently retired to rest between clean sheets, safe in Toad's ancestral home, won back by matchless valour, consummate strategy, and a proper handling of sticks.

The following morning, Toad, who had overslept himself as usual, came down to breakfast disgracefully late, and found on the table a certain quantity of egg-shells, some fragments of cold and leathery toast, a coffee-pot three-fourths empty, and really very little else; which did not tend to improve his temper, considering that, after all, it was his own house. Through the French windows of the breakfast-room he could see the Mole and the Water Rat sitting in wicker-chairs out on the lawn, evidently telling each other stories; roaring with laughter and kicking their short legs up in the air. The Badger, who was in the arm-chair and deep in the morning paper, merely looked up and nodded when Toad entered the room. But Toad knew his man, so he sat down and made the best breakfast he could, merely observing to himself that he would get square with the others sooner or later. When he had nearly finished, the Badger looked up and remarked rather shortly: 'I'm sorry, Toad, but I'm afraid there's a heavy morning's work in front of you. You see, we really ought to have a Banquet at once, to celebrate this affair. It's expected of you—in fact, it's the rule.'

'O, all right!' said the Toad, readily. 'Anything to oblige. Though why on earth you should want to have a Banquet in the morning I cannot understand. But you know I do not live to please myself, but merely to find out what my friends want, and then try and arrange it for 'em, you dear old Badger!'

'Don't pretend to be stupider than you really are,' replied the Badger, crossly; 'and don't chuckle and splutter in your coffee while you're talking; it's not manners. What I mean is, the Banquet will be at night, of course, but the invitations will have to be written and got off at once, and you've got to write 'em. Now, sit down at that table—there's stacks of letter-paper on it, with "Toad Hall" at the top in blue and gold—and write invitations to all our friends, and if you stick to it we shall get them out before luncheon. And *I'll* bear a hand, too, and take my share of the burden. *I'll* order the Banquet.'

'What!' cried Toad, dismayed. 'Me stop indoors and write a lot of rotten letters on a jolly morning like this, when I want to go around my property, and set everything and everybody to rights, and swagger about and enjoy myself! Certainly not! I'll be—I'll see you——Stop a minute, though! Why, of course, dear Badger! What is my pleasure or convenience compared with that of others! You wish it done, and it shall be done. Go, Badger, order the Banquet, order what you like; then join our young friends outside in their innocent mirth, oblivious of me and my cares and toils. I sacrifice this fair morning on the altar of duty and friendship!'

The Badger looked at him very suspiciously, but Toad's frank, open countenance made it difficult to suggest any unworthy motive in this change of attitude. He quitted the room, accordingly, in the direction of the kitchen, and as soon as the door had closed behind him, Toad hurried to the writing-table. A fine idea had occurred to him while he was talking. He *would* write the invitations; and he would take care to mention the leading part he had taken in the fight, and how he had laid the Chief Weasel flat; and he would hint at his adventures, and what a career of triumph he had to tell about; and on the fly-leaf he would set out a sort of a programme of entertainment for the evening—something like this, as he sketched it out in his head:—

SPEECH . . . . BY TOAD
(There will be other speeches by TOAD during the evening.)

ADDRESS . . . . . . BY TOAD
SYNOPSIS—Our Prison System—the Waterways of Old England—Horse-dealing, and how to deal—Property, its rights and its duties—Back to the Land—A Typical English Squire.

SONG . . . . BY TOAD
(*Composed by himself.*)

OTHER COMPOSITIONS . . BY TOAD
will be sung in the course of the evening by the . . . COMPOSER.

The idea pleased him mightily, and he worked very hard and got all the letters finished by noon, at which hour it was reported to him that there was a small and rather bedraggled weasel at the door, inquiring timidly whether he could be of any service to the gentlemen. Toad swaggered out and found it was one of the prisoners of the previous evening, very respectful and anxious to please. He patted him on the head, shoved the bundle of invitations into his paw, and told him to cut along quick and deliver them as fast as he could, and if he liked to come back again in the evening, perhaps there might be a shilling for him, or again, perhaps there mightn't; and the poor weasel seemed really quite grateful, and hurried off eagerly to do his mission.

When the other animals came back to luncheon, very boisterous and breezy after a morning on the river, the Mole, whose conscience had been pricking him, looked doubtfully at Toad, expecting to find him sulky or depressed. Instead, he was so uppish and inflated that the Mole began to suspect something; while the Rat and the Badger exchanged significant glances.

As soon as the meal was over, Toad thrust his paws deep into his trouser-pockets, remarked casually, 'Well, look after yourselves, you fellows! Ask for anything you want!' and was swaggering off in the direction of the garden, where he wanted to think out an idea or two for his coming speeches, when the Rat caught him by the arm.

Toad rather suspected what he was after, and did his best to get away; but when the Badger took him firmly by the other arm he began to see that the game was up. The two animals conducted him between them into the small smoking-room that opened out of the entrance-hall, shut the door, and put him into a chair. Then they both stood in front of him, while Toad sat silent and regarded them with much suspicion and ill-humour.

'Now, look here, Toad,' said the Rat. 'It's about this Banquet, and very sorry I am to have to speak to you like this. But we want you to understand clearly, once and for all, that there are going to be no speeches and no songs. Try and grasp the fact that on this occasion we're not arguing with you; we're just telling you.'

Toad saw that he was trapped. They understood him, they saw through him, they had got ahead of him. His pleasant dream was shattered.

'Mayn't I sing them just one *little* song?' he pleaded piteously.

'No, not *one* little song,' replied the Rat firmly, though his heart bled as he noticed the trembling lip of the poor disappointed Toad. 'It's no good,

Toady; you know well that your songs are all conceit and boasting and vanity; and your speeches are all self-praise and—and—well, and gross exaggeration and—and——'

'And gas,' put in the Badger, in his common way.

'It's for your own good, Toady,' went on the Rat. 'You know you *must* turn over a new leaf sooner or later, and now seems a splendid time to begin; a sort of turning-point in your career. Please don't think that saying all this doesn't hurt me more than it hurts you.'

Toad remained a long while plunged in thought. At last he raised his head, and the traces of strong emotion were visible on his features. 'You have conquered, my friends,' he said in broken accents. 'It was, to be sure, but a small thing that I asked—merely leave to blossom and expand for yet one more evening, to let myself go and hear the tumultuous applause that always seems to me—somehow—to bring out my best qualities. However, you are right, I know, and I am wrong. Henceforth I will be a very different Toad. My friends, you shall never have occasion to blush for me again. But, O dear, O dear, this is a hard world!'

And, pressing his handkerchief to his face, he left the room, with faltering footsteps.

'Badger,' said the Rat, '*I* feel like a brute; I wonder what *you* feel like?'

'O, I know, I know,' said the Badger gloomily. 'But the thing had to be done. This good fellow has got to live here, and hold his own, and be respected. Would you have him a common laughing-stock, mocked and jeered at by stoats and weasels?'

'Of course not,' said the Rat. 'And, talking of weasels, it's lucky we came upon that little weasel, just as he was setting out with Toad's invitations. I suspected something from what you told me, and had a look at one or two; they were simply disgraceful. I confiscated the lot, and the good Mole is now sitting in the blue *boudoir,* filling up plain, simple invitation cards.'

* * *

At last the hour for the banquet began to draw near, and Toad, who on leaving the others had retired to his bedroom, was still sitting there, melancholy and thoughtful. His brow resting on his paw, he pondered long and deeply. Gradually his countenance cleared, and he began to smile long, slow smiles. Then he took to giggling in a shy, self-conscious manner. At last he got up, locked the door, drew the curtains across the windows, collected all the chairs in the room and arranged them in a semicircle, and took up his position in front of them, swelling visibly. Then he bowed, coughed twice, and, letting himself go, with uplifted voice he sang, to the enraptured audience that his imagination so clearly saw,

TOAD'S LAST LITTLE SONG!

The Toad—came—home!
There was panic in the parlours and
howling in the halls,
There was crying in the cow-sheds and
shrieking in the stalls,
When the Toad—came—home!

When the Toad—came—home!
There was smashing in of window and
crashing in of door,
There was chivvying of weasels that
fainted on the floor,
When the Toad—came—home!

Bang! go the drums!
The trumpeters are tooting and the
soldiers are saluting,
And the cannon they are shooting
and the motorcars are hooting,
As the—Hero—comes!

Shout—Hoo-ray!
And let each one of the crowd try and
shout it very loud,
In honour of an animal of whom
you're justly proud,
For it's Toad's—great—day!

He sang this very loud, with great unction and expression; and when he had done, he sang it all over again.

Then he heaved a deep sigh; a long, long, long sigh.

Then he dipped his hairbrush in the waterjug, parted his hair in the middle, and plastered it down very straight and sleek on each side of his face; and, unlocking the door, went quietly down the stairs to greet his guests, who he knew must be assembling in the drawing-room.

All the animals cheered when he entered, and crowded round to congratulate him and say nice things about his courage, and his cleverness, and his fighting qualities; but Toad only smiled faintly, and murmured, 'Not at all!' Or, sometimes, for a change, 'On the contrary!' Otter, who was standing on the hearthrug, describing to an admiring circle of friends exactly how he would have managed things had he been there, came forward with a shout, threw his arm round Toad's neck, and tried to take him round the room in triumphal progress; but Toad, in a mild way, was rather snubby to him, remarking gently, as he disengaged himself, 'Badger's was the mastermind; the Mole and the Water Rat bore the brunt of the fighting; I merely served in the ranks and did little or nothing.' The animals were evidently puzzled and taken aback by this unexpected attitude of his; and Toad felt, as he moved from one guest to the other, making his modest responses, that he was an object of absorbing interest to every one.

The Badger had ordered everything of the best, and the banquet was a great success. There was much talking and laughter and chaff among the animals, but through it all Toad, who of course was in the chair, looked down his nose and murmured pleasant nothings to the animals on either side of him. At intervals he stole a glance at the Badger and the Rat, and always when he looked they were staring at each other with their mouths open; and this gave him the greatest satisfaction. Some of the younger and livelier animals, as the evening wore on, got whispering to each other that things were not so amusing as they used to be in the good old days; and there were some knockings on the table and cries of 'Toad! Speech! Speech from Toad!

Song! Mr. Toad's song!' But Toad only shook his head gently, raised one paw in mild protest, and, by pressing delicacies on his guests, by topical small-talk, and by earnest inquiries after members of their families not yet old enough to appear at social functions, managed to convey to them that this dinner was being run on strictly conventional lines.

He was indeed an altered Toad!

* * *

After this climax, the four animals continued to lead their lives, so rudely broken in upon by civil war, in great joy and contentment, undisturbed by further risings or invasions. Toad, after due consultation with his friends, selected a handsome gold chain and locket set with pearls, which he dispatched to the gaoler's daughter with a letter that even the Badger admitted to be modest, grateful, and appreciative; and the engine-driver, in his turn, was properly thanked and compensated for all his pains and trouble. Under severe compulsion from the Badger, even the barge-woman was, with some trouble, sought out and the value of her horse discreetly made good to her; though Toad kicked terribly at this, holding himself to be an instrument of Fate, sent to punish fat women with mottled arms who couldn't tell a real gentleman when they saw one. The amount involved, it was true, was not very burdensome, the gipsy's valuation being admitted by local assessors or to be approximately correct.

Sometimes, in the course of long summer evenings, the friends would take a stroll together in the Wild Wood, now successfully tamed so far as they were concerned; and it was pleasing to see how respectfully they were greeted by the inhabitants, and how the mother-weasels would bring their young ones to the mouths of their holes, and say, pointing, 'Look, baby! There goes the great Mr. Toad! And that's the gallant Water Rat, a terrible fighter, walking along o' him! And yonder comes the famous Mr. Mole, of whom you so often have heard your father tell!' But when their infants were fractious and quite beyond control, they would quiet them by telling how, if they didn't hush them and not fret them, the terrible grey Badger would up and get them. This was a base libel on Badger, who, though he cared little about society, was rather fond of children; but it never failed to have its full effect.

ALL SUMMER IN A DAY

"READY?"

"Ready."

"Now?"

"Soon."

"Do the scientists really know? Will it happen today, will it?"

"Look, look; see for yourself!"

The children pressed to each other like so many roses, so many weeds, intermixed, peering out for a look at the hidden sun.

It rained.

It had been raining for seven years; thousands upon thousands of days compounded and filled from one end to the other with rain, with the drum and gush of water, with the sweet crystal fall of showers and the concussion of storms so heavy they were tidal waves come over the islands. A thousand forests had been crushed under the rain and grown up a thousand times to be crushed again. And this was the way life was forever on the planet Venus, and this was the schoolroom of the children of the rocket men and women who had come to a raining world to set up civilization and live out their lives.

"It's stopping, it's stopping!"

"Yes, yes!"

Margot stood apart from them, from these children who could never remember a time when there wasn't rain and rain and rain. They were all nine years old, and if there had been a day, seven years ago, when the sun came out for an hour and showed its face to the stunned world, they could not recall. Sometimes, at night, she heard them stir, in remembrance, and she knew they were dreaming and remembering gold or a yellow crayon or a coin large enough to buy the world with. She knew they thought they remembered a warmness, like a blushing in the face, in the body, in the arms and legs and trembling hands. But then they always awoke to the tatting drum, the endless shaking down of clear bead necklaces upon the roof, the walk, the gardens, the forests, and their dreams were gone.

All day yesterday they had read in class about the sun. About how like a lemon it was, and how hot. And they had written small stories or essays about it:

I think the sun is a flower,
That blooms for just one hour.

That was Margot's poem, read in a quiet voice in the still classroom while the rain was falling outside.

"Aw, you didn't write that!" protested one of the boys.

"I did," said Margot. "I *did*."

"William!" said the teacher.

But that was yesterday. Now the rain was slackening, and the children were crushed in the great thick windows.

"Where's teacher?"

"She'll be back."

"She'd better hurry, we'll miss it!"

They turned on themselves, like a feverish wheel, all tumbling spokes.

Margot stood alone. She was a very frail girl who looked as if she had been lost in the rain for years and the rain had washed out the blue from her eyes and the red from her mouth and the yellow from her hair. She was an old photograph dusted from an album, whitened away, and if she spoke at all her voice would be a ghost. Now she stood, separate, staring at the rain and the loud wet world beyond the huge glass.

"What're *you* looking at?" said William.

Margot said nothing.

"Speak when you're spoken to." He gave her a shove. But she did not move; rather she let herself be moved only by him and nothing else.

They edged away from her, they would not look at her. She felt them go away. And this was because she would play no games with them in the echoing tunnels of the underground city. If they tagged her and ran, she stood blinking after them and did not follow. When the class sang songs about happiness and life and games her lips barely moved. Only when they sang about the sun and the summer did her lips move as she watched the drenched windows.

And then, of course, the biggest crime of all was that she had come here only five years ago from Earth, and she remembered the sun and the way the sun was and the sky was when she was four in Ohio. And they, they had been on Venus all their lives, and they had been only two years old when last the sun came out and had long since forgotten the color and heat of it and the way it really was. But Margot remembered.

"It's like a penny," she said once, eyes closed.

"No it's not!" the children cried.

"It's like a fire," she said, "in the stove."

"You're lying, you don't remember!" cried the children.

But she remembered and stood quietly apart from all of them and watched the patterning windows. And once, a month ago, she had refused to shower in the school shower rooms, had clutched her hands to her ears and over her head, screaming the water mustn't touch her head. So after that, dimly, dimly, she sensed it, she was different and they knew her difference and kept away.

There was talk that her father and mother were taking her back to Earth next year; it seemed vital to her that they do so, though it would mean the loss of thousands of dollars to her family. And so, the children hated her for all these reasons of big and little consequence. They hated her pale snow face, her waiting silence, her thinness, and her possible future.

"Get away!" The boy gave her another push. "What're you waiting for?"

Then, for the first time, she turned and looked at him. And what she was waiting for was in her eyes.

"Well, don't wait around here!" cried the boy savagely. "You won't see nothing!"

Her lips moved.

"Nothing!" he cried. "It was all a joke, wasn't it?" He turned to the other children. "Nothing's happening today. *Is it*?"

They all blinked at him and then, understanding, laughed and shook their heads. "Nothing, nothing!"

"Oh, but," Margot whispered, her eyes helpless. "But this is the day, the scientists predict, they say, they *know*, the sun..."

"All a joke!" said the boy, and seized her roughly. "Hey, everyone, let's put her in a closet before teacher comes!"

"No," said Margot, falling back.

They surged about her, caught her up and bore her, protesting and then pleading, and then crying, back into a tunnel, a room, a closet, where they slammed and locked the door. They stood looking at the door and saw it tremble from her beating and throwing herself against it. They heard her muffled cries. Then, smiling, they turned and went out and back down the tunnel, just as the teacher arrived.

"Ready, children?" She glanced at her watch.

"Yes!" said everyone.

"Are we all here?"

"Yes!"

The rain slackened still more.

They crowded to the huge door.

The rain stopped.

It was as if, in the midst of a film concerning an avalanche, a tornado, a hurricane, a volcanic eruption, something had, first, gone wrong with the sound apparatus, thus muffling and finally cutting off all noise, all of the blasts and repercussions and thunders, and then, second, ripped the film from the projector and inserted in its place a peaceful tropical slide which did not move or tremor. The world ground to a standstill. The silence was so immense and unbelievable that you felt your ears had been stuffed or you had lost your hearing altogether. The children put their hands to their ears. They stood apart. The door slid back and the smell of the silent, waiting world came in to them.

The sun came out.

It was the color of flaming bronze and it was very large. And the sky around it was a blazing blue tile color. And the jungle burned with sunlight as the children, released from their spell, rushed out, yelling, into the springtime.

"Now, don't go too far," called the teacher after them. "You've only two hours, you know. You wouldn't want to get caught out!"

But they were running and turning their

faces up to the sky and feeling the sun on their cheeks like a warm iron; they were taking off their jackets and letting the sun burn their arms.

"Oh, it's better than the sun lamps, isn't it?"

"Much, much better!"

They stopped running and stood in the great jungle that covered Venus, that grew and never stopped growing, tumultuously, even as you watched it. It was a nest of octopi, clustering up great arms of fleshlike weed, wavering, flowering in this brief spring. It was the color of rubber and ash, this jungle, from the many years without sun. It was the color of stones and white cheeses and ink, and it was the color of the moon.

The children lay out, laughing, on the jungle mattress, and heard it sigh and squeak under them, resilient and alive. They ran among the trees, they slipped and fell, they pushed each other, they played hide-and-seek and tag, but most of all they squinted at the sun until tears ran down their faces, they put their hands up to that yellowness and that amazing blueness and they breathed of the fresh, fresh air and listened to the silence which suspended them in a blessed sea of no sound and no motion. They looked at everything and savored everything. Then, wildly, like animals escaped from their caves, they ran and ran in shouting circles. They ran for an hour and did not stop running.

And then—

In the midst of their running one of the girls wailed.

Everyone stopped.

The girl, standing in the open, held out her hand.

"Oh, look, look," she said trembling.

They came slowly to look at her opened palm.

In the center of it, cupped and huge, was a single raindrop.

She began to cry, looking at it.

They glanced quietly at the sky.

"Oh. Oh"

A few cold drops fell on their noses and their cheeks and their mouths. The sun faded behind a stir of mist. A wind blew cool around them. They turned and started to walk back toward the underground house, their hands at their sides, their smiles vanishing away.

A boom of thunder startled them and like leaves before a new hurricane, they tumbled upon each other and ran. Lightning struck ten miles away, five miles away, a mile, a half mile. The sky darkened into midnight in a flash.

They stood in the doorway of the underground for a moment until it was raining hard. Then they closed the door and heard the gigantic sound of the rain falling in tons and avalanches, everywhere and forever.

"Will it be seven more years?"

"Yes. Seven."

Then one of them gave a little cry.

"Margot!"

"What?"

"She's still in the closet where we locked her."

"Margot."

They stood as if someone had driven them, like so many stakes, into the floor. They looked at each other and then looked away. They glanced out at the world that was raining now and raining and raining steadily. They could not meet each other's glances. Their faces were solemn and pale. They looked at their hands and feet, their faces down.

"Margot."

One of the girls said, "Well...?"

No one moved.

"Go on," whispered the girl.

They walked slowly down the hall in the

sound of cold rain. They turned through the doorway to the room in the sound of the storm and thunder, lightning on their faces, blue and terrible. They walked over to the closet door slowly and stood by it.

Behind the closet door was only silence.

They unlocked the door, even more slowly, and let Margot out.

THE PIED PIPER OF HAMELIN

Hamelin Town's in Brunswick,
By famous Hanover city;
The river Weser, deep and wide,
Washes its wall on the southern side;
A pleasanter spot you never spied;
But, when begins my ditty,
Almost five hundred years ago,
To see the townsfolk suffer so
From vermin was a pity.

Rats!
They fought the dogs, and kill'd the cats,
And bit the babies in the cradles,
And ate the cheeses out of the vats,
And lick'd the soup from the cook's own ladles,
Split open the kegs of salted sprats,
Made nests inside men's Sunday hats,
And even spoil'd the women's chats,
By drowning their speaking
With shrieking and squeaking
In fifty different sharps and flats.

At last the people in a body
To the Town Hall came flocking:
" 'Tis clear," cried they, "our Mayor's a noddy;
And as for our Corporation—shocking
To think we buy gowns lined with ermine
For dolts that can't or won't determine
What's best to rid us of our vermin!

You hope, because you're old and obese,
To find in the furry civic robe ease?
Rouse up, sirs! Give your brains a racking
To find the remedy we're lacking,
Or, sure as fate, we'll send you packing!"
At this the Mayor and Corporation
Quaked with a mighty consternation.
An hour they sate in counsel,
  At length the Mayor broke silence:
"For a guilder I'd my ermine gown sell;
  I wish I were a mile hence!
It's easy to bid one rack one's brain—
I'm sure my poor head aches again,
I've scratch'd it so, and all in vain.
Oh for a trap, a trap, a trap!"
Just as he said this, what should hap
At the chamber-door but a gentle tap?
"Bless us!" cried the Mayor, "what's that?"
(With the Corporation as he sat,
Looking little though wondrous fat;
Nor brighter was his eye, nor moister
Than a too long-open'd oyster,
Save when at noon his paunch grew mutinous
For a plate of turtle, green and glutinous)
"Only a scraping of shoes on the mat?
Anything like the sound of a rat
Makes my heart go pit-a-pat!"

"Come in!"—the Mayor cried, looking bigger:
And in did come the strangest figure!
His queer long coat from heel to head
Was half of yellow and half of red;
And he himself was tall and thin,

With sharp blue eyes, each like a pin,
And light loose hair, yet swarthy skin,
No tuft on cheek nor beard on chin,
But lips where smiles went out and in—
There was no guessing his kith and kin!
And nobody could enough admire
The tall man and his quaint attire:
Quoth one: "It's as if my great-grandsire,
Starting up at the Trump of Doom's tone,
Had walk'd this way from his painted tombstone!"

He advanced to the council-table:
And, "Please your honors," said he, "I'm able,
By means of a secret charm, to draw
All creatures living beneath the sun,
That creep, or swim, or fly, or run,
After me so as you never saw!
And I chiefly use my charm
On creatures that do people harm,
The mole, and toad, and newt, and viper;
And people call me the Pied Piper."
(And here they noticed round his neck
A scarf of red and yellow stripe,
To match with his coat of the selfsame check;
And at the scarf's end hung a pipe;
And his fingers, they noticed, were ever straying
As if impatient to be playing
Upon this pipe, as low it dangled
Over his vesture so old-fangled.)
"Yet," said he, "poor piper as I am,
In Tartary I freed the Cham,
Last June, from his huge swarm of gnats;
I eased in Asia the Nizam

Of a monstrous brood of vampyre bats;
And, as for what your brain bewilders—
If I can rid your town of rats,
Will you give me a thousand guilders?"
"One? fifty thousand!" was the exclamation
Of the astonish'd Mayor and Corporation.

Into the street the Piper stept,
  Smiling first a little smile,
As if he knew what magic slept
  In his quiet pipe the while;
Then, like a musical adept,
To blow the pipe his lips he wrinkled,
And green and blue his sharp eyes twinkled,
Like a candle-flame where salt is sprinkled;
And ere three shrill notes the pipe had utter'd,
You heard as if an army mutter'd;
And the muttering grew to a grumbling;
And the grumbling grew to a mighty rumbling;
And out of the houses the rats came tumbling.
Great rats, small rats, lean rats, brawny rats,
Brown rats, black rats, gray rats, tawny rats,
Grave old plodders, gay young friskers,
  Fathers, mothers, uncles, cousins,
Cocking tails and prickling whiskers,
  Families by tens and dozens,
Brothers, sisters, husbands, wives—
Follow'd the Piper for their lives.
From street to street he piped advancing,
And step for step they follow'd dancing,
Until they came to the river Weser,
Wherein all plunged and perish'd,
Save one who, stout as Julius Cæsar,
Swam across and lived to carry

(As the manuscript he cherish'd)
To Rat-land home his commentary,
Which was, "At the first shrill notes of the pipe,
I heard a sound as of scraping tripe,
And putting apples, wondrous ripe,
Into a cider press's gripe:
And a moving away of pickle-tub boards,
And a leaving ajar of conserve-cupboards,
And a drawing the corks of train-oil flasks,
And a breaking the hoops of butter-casks;
And it seemed as if a voice
(Sweeter far than by harp or by psaltery
Is breathed) call'd out, O rats, rejoice!
The world is grown to one vast dry-saltery!
So munch on, crunch on, take your nuncheon,
Breakfast, supper, dinner, luncheon!
And just as a bulky sugar-puncheon,
All ready staved, like a great sun shone
Glorious scarce an inch before me,
Just as methought it said, Come, bore me!
I found the Weser rolling o'er me."

You should have heard the Hamelin people
Ringing the bells till they rock'd the steeple;
"Go," cried the Mayor, "and get long poles!
Poke out the nests and block up the holes!
Consult with carpenters and builders,
And leave in our town not even a trace
Of the rats!"—when suddenly up the face
Of the Piper perk'd in the market-place,
With a, "First, if you please, my thousand guilders!"

A thousand guilders! The Mayor look'd blue;
So did the Corporation too.

For council dinners made rare havoc
With Claret, Moselle, Vin-de-Grave, Hock;
And half the money would replenish
Their cellar's biggest butt with Rhenish.
To pay this sum to a wandering fellow
With a gypsy coat of red and yellow!
"Beside," quoth the Mayor, with a knowing wink,
"Our business was done at the river's brink;
We saw with our eyes the vermin sink,
And what's dead can't come to life, I think.
So, friend, we're not the folks to shrink
From the duty of giving you something for drink,
And a matter of money to put in your poke;
But, as for the guilders, what we spoke
Of them, as you very well know, was in joke.
Beside, our losses have made us thrifty;
A thousand guilders! Come, take fifty!"

The Piper's face fell and he cried,
"No trifling! I can't wait! beside,
I've promised to visit by dinner-time
Bagdad, and accept the prime
Of the Head Cook's pottage, all he's rich in,
For having left, in the Caliph's kitchen,
Of a nest of scorpions no survivor—
With him I proved no bargain-driver.
With you, don't think I'll bate a stiver!
And folks who put me in a passion
May find me pipe to another fashion."

"How?" cried the Mayor, "d'ye think I'll brook
Being worse treated than a Cook?
Insulted by a lazy ribald

With idle pipe and vesture piebald?
You threaten us, fellow? Do your worst,
Blow your pipe there till you burst!"

Once more he stept into the street;
  And to his lips again
Laid his long pipe of smooth straight cane;
  And ere he blew three notes (such sweet
Soft notes as yet musician's cunning
  Never gave the enraptured air)
There was a rustling, that seem'd like a bustling
Of merry crowds justling at pitching and hustling,
Small feet were pattering, wooden shoes clattering,
Little hands clapping, and little tongues chattering,
And, like fowls in a farm-yard when barley is scattering,
Out came the children running.
All the little boys and girls,
With rosy cheeks and flaxen curls,
And sparkling eyes and teeth like pearls,
Tripping and skipping, ran merrily after
The wonderful music with shouting and laughter.

The Mayor was dumb, and the Council stood
As if they were changed into blocks of wood,
Unable to move a step, or cry
To the children merrily skipping by—
And could only follow with the eye
That joyous crowd at the Piper's back.
But how the Mayor was on the rack,
And the wretched Council's bosoms beat,
As the Piper turn'd from the High Street
To where the Weser roll'd its waters
Right in the way of their sons and daughters!

However, he turned from south to west,
And to Koppelberg Hill his steps address'd,
And after him the children press'd;
Great was the joy in every breast.
"He never can cross that mighty top!
He's forced to let the piping drop,
And we shall see our children stop!"
When, lo, as they reach'd the mountain's side,
A wondrous portal open'd wide,
As if a cavern was suddenly hollow'd;
And the Piper advanced and the children follow'd,
And when all were in to the very last,
The door in the mountain-side shut fast.
Did I say all? No! one was lame,
And could not dance the whole of the way,
And in after years, if you would blame
His sadness, he was used to say,
"It's dull in our town since my playmates left!
I can't forget that I'm bereft
Of all the pleasant sights they see,
Which the Piper also promised me,
For he led us, he said, to a joyous land,
Joining the town and just at hand,
Where waters gush'd and fruit trees grew,
And flowers put forth a fairer hue,
And everything was strange and new;
The sparrows were brighter than peacocks here,
And the dogs outran our fallow deer,
And honey-bees had lost their stings,
And horses were born with eagles' wings;
And just as I became assured
My lame foot would be speedily cured,
The music stopp'd, and I stood still,

And found myself outside the Hill,
Left alone against my will,
To go now limping as before,
And never hear of that country more!"

Alas, alas for Hamelin!
  There came into many a burgher's pate
  A text which says that Heaven's Gate
  Opes to the rich at as easy rate
As the needle's eye takes a camel in!
The Mayor sent east, west, north, and south
To offer the Piper by word of mouth,
  Wherever it was men's lot to find him,
Silver and gold to his heart's content,
If he'd only return the way he went,
  And bring the children behind him.
But when they saw 'twas a lost endeavor,
And Piper and dancers were gone forever,
They made a decree that lawyers never
  Should think their records dated duly
If, after the day of the month and year,
These words did not as well appear:
"And so long after what happen'd here
  On the twenty-second of July,
Thirteen hundred and Seventy-six;"
And the better in memory to fix
The place of the children's last retreat,
They call'd it the Pied Piper's Street,
Where any one playing on pipe or tabor
Was sure for the future to lose his labor.
Nor suffer'd they hostelry or tavern
  To shock with mirth a street so solemn,
But opposite the place of the cavern

They wrote the story on a column,
And on the great church-window painted
The same, to make the world acquainted
How their children were stolen away,
And there it stands to this very day.
And I must not omit to say
That in Transylvania there's a tribe
Of alien people that ascribe
The outlandish ways and dress
On which their neighbors lay such stress,
To their fathers and mothers having risen
Out of some subterranean prison,
Into which they were trepann'd
Long time ago in a mighty band
Out of Hamelin town in Brunswick land,
But how or why, they don't understand.

So, Willy, let you and me be wipers
Of scores out with all men—especially pipers;
And, whether they pipe us free, from rats or from mice,
If we've promised them aught, let us keep our promise.

MAURICE'S ROOM

1. THE COLLECTION

Maurice's room measured six long steps in one direction and five in the other. The distance from the floor to the ceiling was three times higher than Maurice. There was one window through which Maurice could see several other windows as well as a piece of the sky. From the middle of the ceiling dangled a long string, the kind used to tie up packages of laundry. Attached to the end of the string was a dried octopus. It was the newest addition to Maurice's collection. When his mother or father walked into his room—which wasn't often—the octopus swung back and forth a little in the draught.

Maurice had used a ladder to climb up high enough to tack the string to the ceiling. The ladder was still leaning against the wall. Instead of returning it to Mr. Klenk, the janitor of his building, from whom he had borrowed it, Maurice was using the steps for shelves. Even though Maurice's father, Mr. Henry, had put up a dozen shelves around the room for all of Maurice's things, there still weren't enough.

Maurice knew how to walk around his room without stepping on anything, and so did his friend Jacob. But no one else did.

As his mother and father often said to visitors, it was astonishing how much junk a person could find in one city block. His mother said Maurice kept their block clean because he brought up everything from the street to his room. His father said Maurice ought to get a salary from the Department of Sanitation because of all the work he was doing in cleaning up the city. At least once a month Mr. and Mrs. Henry talked about moving to the country. It would be better for Maurice, they said. But then they would decide to wait a little longer.

Some visitors said that collections like Maurice's showed that a child would become a great scientist. Many great scientists had collected junk when they were eight years old. Other visitors said Maurice would outgrow his collection and become interested in other things, such as money or armies. Some suggested to the Henrys that they ought to buy Maurice a dog, or send him to music school so that his time might be spent more usefully.

In his room Maurice had a bottle full of dead beetles, a powdery drift of white moths in a cup without a handle, a squirrel hide tacked to a board, a snakeskin on a wire hanger, a raccoon tail, a glass of shrimp eggs, a plate of mealy worms, a box of turtle food.

There were things with which to make other things, such as nails of different sizes, screws, wire, butterfly bolts, scraps of wood, sockets, filaments from electric-light bulbs, cardboard from grocery boxes, two orange crates, a handsaw and a hammer. On the top of a chest of drawers Maurice kept stones and pebbles, dried tar balls, fragments of brick, pieces of colored bottle glass that had been worn smooth, and gray rocks that glistened with mica.

On his window sill there was a heap of dried moss next to a turtle bowl in which several salamanders lived half hidden by mud and wet grass. On the same sill he kept some plants from the five-and-ten-cent store. They looked dead. Now and then a cactus would put out a new shoot.

In another bowl on a table covered with

yellow oilcloth were four painted turtles that were getting quite soft in the shell, and in a corner, in a square fish bowl with a chicken-wire roof, lived a garter snake and a lizard. An old hamster in his cage slept or filled his pouches with dried carrots or ran on his wheel. The wheel, which needed an oiling, screeched all night, the time the hamster preferred for exercise. But the noise didn't keep Maurice awake, only his parents. In a pickle jar, a garden spider sat in a forked twig, her egg sack just below her. Maurice also had a bird. It was a robin, blind in one eye and unable to find food for itself.

On the floor were coffee cans with things in them; an eggbeater with a missing gear, a pile of dead starfish, cigar boxes, clockworks, hinges, and a very large grater with sharp dents on all four of its sides. The grater was orange with rust, and it stood in the middle of the room beneath the octopus. You would have to use a magnifying glass to see all the other things Maurice had found.

His bed had two blankets and a pillow without a pillowcase. Sometimes a small goose feather pricked its way through the ticking, and Maurice would put it away in an envelope. He had used two pillowcases for his collecting expeditions, and after that his mother wouldn't give him any more.

There was one tidy corner in Maurice's room. It was where he had pushed his Christmas toys. They were a month old now, and the dust covered them evenly. They were like furniture or bathroom fixtures. Maurice felt there wasn't much to be done with them.

2. "GET EVERYTHING OFF THE FLOOR"

It was the end of January, and Maurice had just come home from school. He put his books on his bed and went to see what the snake was doing. It was lying on its rock. The lizard was watching it. The robin was so still it looked stuffed. But it cocked its head when Maurice whistled at it. The hamster was hiding bits of carrot in the sawdust at the bottom of its cage. The salamanders had buried themselves in the mud. Maurice was arranging little piles of food for his animals when he heard his uncle's voice from down the hall.

"Lily," his uncle was saying to his mother, "you ought to dynamite that room!"

"There must be another way," his mother

said.

"You'd better give it up," said his uncle. "Maurice will never clean it."

"If we lived in the country, it would be different," said his mother.

"Perhaps," said his uncle.

Maurice took two walnuts from his pocket and cracked them together. His mother came to the door.

"Get everything off the floor," she said in a low, even voice as though she were counting moving freight cars.

"Where will I put things?" asked Maurice.

"I don't care," she said. "But clear the floor! Or else I'll bring in the broom, the dustpan, and a very large box. And that will be that!"

The doorbell rang. It was Jacob.

"Jacob can help you," his mother said.

Jacob was seven, but he looked bigger than Maurice. It was because he was wearing so many clothes—scarves, mittens, sweaters, two hats, and several pairs of socks. He began to take off his outer clothing, laying each item in a pile at his feet. Meanwhile Maurice explained the predicament.

"What are we going to do?" asked Jacob.

Maurice looked at the chest of drawers. The pebbles and rocks had been moved to the floor, and the chest was now covered with oatmeal boxes. He looked at the table. He could barely see the yellow oilcloth because it was hidden by sections of a witch doctor's mask he and Jacob had begun to make the week before. The turtles had been moved next to the salamanders on the window sill.

"There are five more floors in this room if you count the walls and ceiling," Maurice said to Jacob. Jacob looked smaller and thinner now that he was down to his shirt and pants.

"I see," said Jacob.

"We'll have to ask Mr. Klenk to help us," said Maurice.

Jacob began to sort out nails. Then he stopped. "But we won't be able to do that with everything! And how can we get it all done in just a day?"

"Mr. Klenk will know," said Maurice.

3. THE JANITOR

Mr. Klenk, the janitor, lived in the basement five floors down. The basement smelled like wet mops, damp cement, pipes, and old furniture stuffing. But it was clean. Mr. Klenk had told Maurice that he couldn't relax a second or he would be drowned by the rubbish that poured out of all the apartments. "Overwhelming!" Mr. Klenk often exclaimed.

"It's a race between me and the junk," he would say. "If I let it get an edge on me, I'll get shoved right out of the city." But Mr. Klenk didn't seem to feel the same way about Maurice's collection.

"Well, you're selective, my boy," he had said once, giving Maurice a caramel. "Besides, I suspect you've got something in mind for all that stuff of yours."

The two boys rang the janitor's bell. Mr. Klenk opened his door, blowing out a cloud of cigar smoke.

"I have to get everything off the floor," Maurice said. "Could you help us a little?"

"What do you have in mind?"

"There's plenty of space on the walls," said Maurice.

Mr. Klenk nodded and puffed on his cigar. "I know," he said. "But you didn't bring back my ladder, did you?"

"He forgot," said Jacob timidly. Mr. Klenk peered through the cigar smoke. Jacob backed away. The janitor in the building where Jacob lived sat in a big collapsed steamer trunk all day just waiting, Jacob was sure, for boys to wander by so he could pounce on them.

"Can you come now?" asked Maurice.

"Let's go," answered Mr. Klenk.

When they reached Maurice's room, Mr. Klenk stopped at the doorway.

"How am I supposed to get in there?" he asked.

Jacob cleared a path for him. Maurice took all the things off the ladder steps, and in a few minutes Mr. Klenk was at work.

First Maurice chose the starfish. He handed it to Jacob, who held it up to Mr. Klenk on the ladder. Next came the rusty grater. In an hour everything was hanging either from the ceiling or from the walls. The animals paid no attention to the fact that they were suspended above the floor. The hamster went to sleep; his cage swung gently like a hammock in a light breeze.

By six o'clock, the floor boards appeared. It was a good floor, and Maurice and Jacob sat down on it.

"Now we have room for more things," said Maurice.

Maurice's mother and his uncle came to the door.

"Wow!" said Uncle.

Mrs. Henry looked pale. "I didn't have *that* in mind," she said.

"Well, Lily, they've cleared the floor," said the uncle. He looked at Maurice. "I have a surprise," he said. "I'm going to bring Patsy here to spend a week with you."

Then his uncle winked at Mrs. Henry. "You'll see," he said to her. "Patsy will take his mind off all of this." Maurice's mother looked doubtful.

"Who is Patsy?" asked Jacob.

"Who is Patsy!" repeated the uncle, as though astonished. "Tell him, Maurice."

"A dog," said Maurice. "A dumb fat dog," he added in a whisper to Jacob.

After Maurice's uncle and Mrs. Henry went back to the kitchen, Mr. Klenk picked up his ladder and started to leave. Then he seemed to remember something. He tapped Maurice on the shoulder.

"Would you like a stuffed bear?" he asked.

"I'd like a bear," Maurice said.

"A tenant left it when he moved out," said Mr. Klenk. "Send your man down for it in the near future." He nodded at Jacob.

"We could make a car for it," said Maurice after Mr. Klenk had left.

"There's a busted baby carriage in front of

my building," said Jacob.

"Bring the wheels," said Maurice.

Jacob began to put on all his outdoor clothes.

"I never heard of a bear having a car," he said.

"Why not?" asked Maurice.

4. THE DOG

Maurice and Jacob were unable to begin building a car for the bear the next day because Patsy arrived early in the morning.

Patsy was a large soft dog with beady eyes. She was wearing a plaid wool coat. Maurice and she stared at each other for several minutes. She was nearly as tall as he was. Then she walked straight into Maurice's room. When she came out a minute later, she had an oatmeal box in her mouth.

"Give me that!" demanded Maurice. Patsy lowered herself slowly on her four legs until she was lying on the floor with the box in her teeth.

Maurice looked at his mother. She was smiling and nodding. He looked at his father who was just about to leave for work.

"Nice dog," said his father.

"Give it back," whispered Maurice to Patsy. She stared at him. Then she turned her head suddenly, and Maurice snatched the oatmeal box and ran to his room with it. He closed the door and went back to the kitchen to finish his bacon and cocoa.

When he came out to put on his galoshes before going to school, Patsy was sitting in the living room. She was chewing an ear section of the witch doctor's mask. He ran to her and grabbed it. Patsy stood up and wagged her tail. Maurice could see she was just waiting for him to leave. He pretended to go to the front door, then suddenly turned and tiptoed back to his room. Patsy was already in it, sniffing up at the hamster.

"Please leave my room," said Maurice. Patsy looked at him over her back. He slipped his fingers beneath her collar and pulled. It was difficult to drag such a big dog. His mother came to the door. "Don't bully the dog," she said. "Good Patsy!"

"I don't want her in my room," said Maurice.

"She's so friendly," his mother said. Patsy wagged her tail and sat down on Maurice's foot.

"She was trying to eat the hamster," Maurice said.

"Oh!" exclaimed his mother. "You're exaggerating! She was only looking around. She probably misses your uncle."

Maurice looked at a round hole in his door near the knob where he and Jacob had dug out the lock and the latch months ago.

"Couldn't we put the lock back in?" he asked.

"Not now," said Mrs. Henry. "Now you go to school. You're going to be late!"

Right after his arithmetic class, Maurice asked the teacher for permission to go to the principal's office. The secretary said he could use the telephone for two minutes.

"Hello," said Maurice's mother.

"Is she in there?" asked Maurice.

"Who?" asked Mrs. Henry.

"Pull the octopus higher," said Maurice.

"Oh, Maurice," said Mrs. Henry, "as if I didn't have enough to do! Patsy doesn't want your octopus."

Maurice looked up at the clock.

"Can't you tie her to something?" Maurice asked.

"Stop fussing," said Mrs. Henry.

After school, Maurice ran all the way home.

He was out of breath when he reached his front door.

Patsy was lying asleep in the living room. Maurice's things were all around her like a fortress. Her head was resting on the racoon tail.

It took Maurice an hour to put everything back. Patsy watched him from the door.

"Thief!" he said to her. She wagged her tail.

The next day Maurice did not feel very well. His mother said he could stay home provided he kept to his bed. "None of this wandering around in bare feet," she said.

Maurice was happy to stay in his room. He watched Patsy as she paced back and forth outside his door. When she tried to sneak in, he shouted, "No, you don't!"

That afternoon he heard his mother speaking with his uncle on the telephone.

"Maurice and Patsy are inseparable," she said. "You were quite right. We must get him a dog of his own."

"A whole week," said Maurice to himself. He began to feel really sick. Suddenly Patsy made a dash for the chest of drawers. She put one paw on a drawer pull.

"Out!" shouted Maurice, standing up in the middle of his bed with the blankets flapping around him. Patsy ran from the room, but she sat down right in front of the door.

The next day Maurice felt poorly again. His mother took his temperature. He had no fever. His throat wasn't red. But his eyes looked strained. The strain came from staring through the dark at Patsy half the night. But the dog had fallen asleep before Maurice had and so she had been unable to steal a single thing from Maurice's room.

"I think you should go to school," said Mrs. Henry.

"No!" said Maurice, kneeling on his bed.

"Mercy! You don't have to kneel," she said. "What *is* the matter?"

"I can't go to school," Maurice said.

Mrs. Henry called Mr. Henry.

"I think he is developing a school phobia," Maurice heard her say to his father as they stood in the hall outside his room.

At that moment, Patsy raced in, threw herself at the bed, snatched a blanket, and made off with it. Maurice jumped to the floor and ran after her. They both slammed into Maurice's father.

"If you don't stop playing with Patsy, I'll have to send her home!" said Mr. Henry.

After that, it was easy. Maurice played with

Patsy every minute he could, and soon his uncle came to get her. He dressed Patsy in her plaid coat, clipped on her leash, put on his hat, and left.

"You see?" said Maurice's father.

Maurice nodded.

5. THE BEAR

One Saturday morning, a few weeks after Patsy had left, Maurice awoke at six o'clock. His window was blurred because it was raining so hard. The hamster stirred in its cage.

"You're up too early," Maurice said. The robin lifted one wing slowly and opened its good eye. Maurice went into the kitchen and made himself a grape-jelly sandwich. It felt good to be eating a sandwich and walking down the hall so early in the morning. No one else was awake. He gave a piece of bread crust to the robin and one to the hamster. Then he got dressed.

Soon there was a soft knock on the front door. It was Jacob, who always arrived early on Saturday mornings and who usually brought something with him. Today he was carrying a paper sack.

"Do you want a jelly sandwich?" asked Maurice. Jacob nodded. Then he showed Maurice what he had brought in the bag.

"What is it?" asked Maurice.

"I think it's for weighing things. I found it in a box on the street," Jacob said, holding up a large white scale. The paint was chipped, and when Maurice pressed his hand down on the platform, the needle on the dial jiggled.

"Your arm weighs six pounds," said Jacob.

Maurice's mother walked by. She was yawning. She glanced into the room. "Good morning, children," she said.

"My arm is very heavy," said Maurice.

"That's nice," said Maurice's mother, and yawned again and walked on.

"I forgot to tell you," Jacob said. "Mr. Klenk said to come and get the bear."

Maurice put the scale on his bed. Then both boys ran to the front door and down the five flights of stairs to Mr. Klenk's room in the basement. Mr. Klenk was blowing on the cup of coffee he was holding in one hand. He still carried a broom in the other.

"It seems I hardly have time for coffee," said Mr. Klenk. "I'll be glad to get rid of that bear."

He left them standing at the door, peering into his room. There was so much cigar smoke in the air, it was hard to see the furniture. In a minute Mr. Klenk was back, pushing the bear before him. The bear's feet were strapped into roller skates. It was as tall as Jacob.

"Here he is," said Mr. Klenk. "Think you can handle him?"

Jacob and Maurice stared. The bear was plump. Its fur was black. Its two front paws stuck out straight in front of it. The claws were of different lengths, and some of them pointed upward as though the bear had been pushing against a wall.

"Why is it wearing skates?" asked Maurice.

"It came that way," said Mr. Klenk.

"It looks tired," said Jacob.

"It had a long sea voyage, all the way from South America."

Maurice pulled and Jacob pushed and they got the bear up the stairs all the way to Maurice's front door, and inside. Because of the skates the bear moved easily on a level surface, but it had been a slippery business getting it up the stairs.

"I think we'd better wait a while before we show it to my mother and father," said Maurice. "They don't like surprises."

"Mine neither," Jacob said.

Maurice said, "Why don't you get your hat and coat and put them on the bear and maybe they'll think it's you if we push him down the hall fast."

Jacob went to get his outdoor clothes. They dressed the bear, pulling Jacob's hat almost all the way down its muzzle. Then, running, they propelled it down the hall. As they went by his parents' bedroom, Maurice's father poked his head around the door.

"Who's that?" asked Mr. Henry in a sleepy voice.

"Jacob!" said Maurice.

"Maurice!" said Jacob.

Mr. Henry went back to bed. "You shouldn't roller-skate in the house," he said.

At last they got the bear into a corner of Maurice's room. "The bear has a funny smell," said Jacob.

"You're right," said Maurice. "But we'll have to get used to it."

They took Jacob's clothes off the bear. Then they stood and looked at it. It was pleasant to have a big animal in the room with them, even if it was stuffed.

"Maurice," Mrs. Henry called. "Come and drink your apple juice."

"We'll have to disguise it. Then one day when they're feeling good I'll just tell them I have a bear," said Maurice in a whisper. Then he called out, "We'll be there in a minute."

"Couldn't we hide it under the bed for a while?" asked Jacob.

"No," said Maurice. "It won't fit because the Victrola's there. But wait a minute." Maurice opened his closet door and pulled out a heap of clothing. Pretty soon he found what he wanted. It was a penguin costume.

"It was for Halloween," said Maurice.

They started dressing the bear. They had to cut holes in the feet to fit the costume over the bear's roller skates. Then they zipped up the front and pushed the bear between the table and the window. Nothing was left showing of it except the big bumps where its paws were.

Then they went to the kitchen and had apple juice and doughnuts.

6. PATSY AGAIN

The next day, which was Sunday, Maurice's uncle was coming to visit. When Maurice heard that Patsy was coming with him, he went to his room and began to pile up things behind his door.

Maurice's father knocked, and Maurice opened the door a crack.

"Maurice," he said, "you'll have to clean out the hamster's cage. There's a very strong smell coming from your room."

"All right," said Maurice. "I'll do it right now."

He looked at the bear in its penguin costume.

"I wonder if I could spray you with perfume," he said.

Then he took a piece of rope and tied one end of it around the bear's neck and the other to his bedpost. If somebody came in, he decided, he would just roll the bear out the window and then pull it back into the room when the coast was clear.

A few minutes later, he heard his mother let his uncle in at the front door.

"Well, Lily, how are you?"

"Fine, and you?"

"Fine, and your husband?"

"Fine, and Patsy?"

"Fine."

"Fine," said Maurice to the hamster.

"And how is Maurice?" asked the uncle.

"Fine," said his mother.

"He'll be delighted to see Patsy."

"He surely will be delighted."

Maurice added his boots to the heap behind his door.

A large object suddenly hurtled down the hall and against Maurice's door. It was Patsy. The barricade gave way, and Patsy raced into the room, stomping and huffing and panting. The snake slid under its rock, the lizard froze, the hamster burrowed in its sawdust, and the bird closed its good eye.

Patsy stopped dead in her tracks. Maurice stood up slowly from where he had been crouching near his bed. Patsy's nose was in the air. She was sniffing. She slid one floppy paw forward, then another. Maurice sprang toward the bear, his arms outstretched.

"Don't lay a hand on that bear!" he cried.

It was too late. Patsy leaped. Over and down crashed the bear. All eight wheels of the roller skates spun in the air. Patsy sat on the bear and began to bay. Maurice could hear his mother, his father, and his uncle racing down the hall.

He ran to the window, flung it open, and deposited the turtles on the floor. He grabbed a blanket from his bed and threw it over Patsy, who fell into a tangled heap alongside the bear. In a flash, Maurice had the bear up on its skates and on the sill. He gave it a shove, and out it went through the window, the rope trailing behind it.

Mr. Klenk, who was sweeping the courtyard below and whistling softly to himself, heard the whir of spinning roller skates and looked up. "Ye gods!" he cried. "A giant penguin!"

7. THE TRUMPET LESSON

"Today you are going to start your trumpet lessons," said Mrs. Henry. She held out a black case that reminded Maurice of a crocodile's head. Maurice put it on his bed and opened it. The trumpet glittered. He could see his face reflected in it.

He looked out of his window. A light rain was falling, a March rain that might be warm. It was exactly the kind of Saturday Maurice and Jacob liked to spend hunting for new things for the collection.

"You'll have to leave very soon," said Mrs. Henry as she started back to the kitchen to finish her cup of coffee. Maurice lifted the snake out of its cage. The snake wound itself around his wrist. It was a dull green color and quite small.

"The trouble with you is you don't have enough interests," he said to the snake. He put it back in its cage and pulled the chicken wire over the top. Then he put on his light jacket.

When he got to the front door, his mother said, "Just a minute. Haven't you forgotten something?" She was holding out the trumpet case. "And Maurice, really! It's raining! Put on your rubbers and your heavy jacket."

"Maurice, you must learn to be more responsible," said his father, who was standing at the other end of the hall eating a piece of whole-wheat toast.

Maurice went back to his room, dug into his closet, and found one of his rubbers and one of Jacob's. He wished he had been born wearing one pair of shoes and one suit of clothes.

Jacob was waiting for him in front of the building.

"Do your lessons really start today?" he asked.

"Yes," said Maurice. As he had guessed, it was a warm spring rain.

"Will you have to go every Saturday morning?"

"For six weeks," said Maurice. "Then they'll see."

"See what?" asked Jacob.

"If I get new interests."

On their way to the music school where Maurice was to take his lesson, they passed a big junk yard. A sign hung over the wire fence that surrounded the yard: *Auto Parts.* A man wearing a hat was walking around the piles of bumpers and tires and car bodies. Now and then he would kick an old fender.

"Why don't you wait for me in there," Maurice suggested. "Maybe you can find something good." The man with the hat walked into a little house not much bigger than a telephone booth. There was a small window in it. Maurice could see the man fiddling with a radio.

"Maybe he'll chase me away," said Jacob, looking at the man.

"I'll stay for a minute," said Maurice.

They walked toward the rear of the lot. The man looked out of his window but didn't seem to see them. He was chewing on a toothpick and still twisting the radio dials. Just behind the little house, Maurice and Jacob could see the long arm of a crane.

"Look at that!" said Maurice, pointing to a

pyramid of heaped-up car parts. Poking out of the pile were hubcaps, fenders, tires, fan belts, radiator caps, pipes, window frames, steering wheels on shafts, and at the very top, lying on a car hood, a pair of headlights that looked almost new.

"We could use those headlights," said Maurice.

Jacob looked back at the little house. "He won't give them to us," he said.

"Maybe he'd make a trade," said Maurice.

"What could we trade?" asked Jacob.

"We'll think of something," Maurice answered. "But first we have to see those headlights."

"How will we get them?" asked Jacob.

"Climb," said Maurice. "See all the places you can put your feet?"

"Me?" asked Jacob.

"I think you can do it better. I'm heavier. If I tried it, everything might crash down," Maurice said.

"Are you going to ask him first if we can?" asked Jacob.

"He's not even looking at us," said Maurice.

Jacob put his right foot on a tire rim, then grabbed hold of the fender above him and brought his left foot up to another tire. Slowly he climbed toward the top, using the tires as steps.

Suddenly there was a loud clanging of metal, then bangs, screeches, and a crash. When the dust cleared, Maurice saw Jacob almost at the top of the pyramid, stretched out on a silver-colored car hood, clutching its sides.

The man ran out of his little house. When he saw Jacob, he threw his hat on the ground.

"What's the meaning of this!" he shouted.

"We'd like to make a trade," said Maurice.

"Trade! At a time like this?" bellowed the man. "Get off my property!"

"Help!" said Jacob in a weak voice.

"How will we get him down?" asked Maurice.

The man picked up his hat and jammed it back on his head. "Can't he fly?" he growled; then he turned and walked to the crane. He jumped up to the seat and began to push the levers around furiously.

"Don't worry," Maurice called up to Jacob. "He's going to get you down."

Jacob didn't answer. He wasn't scared now, and he rather liked being so high above the ground.

There was a grinding of gears and a maniacal roar as the man maneuvered the crane into position.

"Clear away," shouted the man to Maurice. Maurice ran back toward the little house and watched as the claw at the end of the cables lowered its jaw, then clamped onto the hood where Jacob lay, gripped it, and lifted it down slowly like a plate. Several tires dislodged by the crane rolled along the ground.

"Well, get up," said Maurice to Jacob. Jacob was feeling sleepy. He shook himself a little and stood up.

"How was it?" asked Maurice.

"Okay," said Jacob.

The man jumped down from the crane, picked up a tire, and kicked it so hard it rolled all the way back to the pile. Then he started toward them.

Maurice and Jacob hurried to the gate. But Maurice stopped suddenly and darted into the little house, where he placed the trumpet on top of the radio.

"It's too late for my lesson anyhow," he said to Jacob as the man yelled after them, "I've got a friend on the police force!"

On the way home, Jacob said, "What will your mother and father say?"

"Plenty!" said Maurice.

8. A BIRTHDAY PRESENT

In a few weeks Mr. and Mrs. Henry stopped mentioning the trumpet. After that, whenever Maurice happened to hear them, they were talking about moving to the country. "We'll have to move anyway, at the rate Maurice is going," Mrs. Henry said once. "If he puts one more thing in his room, he won't have a place to stand."

But Mr. Henry wanted to wait.

On a morning late in April, Mrs. Henry brought Maurice a glass of fresh orange juice on a little tray. There was a sign leaning against the glass. It read: "Happy Birthday to Maurice." She couldn't get into the room so Maurice got up from his bed and went to the door to get the tray.

Jacob came at noon and they had a birthday lunch. Maurice blew out all of his nine candles but he forgot to make a wish. Then Mr. and Mrs. Henry brought in a large box.

Maurice looked inside. It was a three-foot-long sailboat. The rigging was made of cord. The sails were of canvas, the winches really turned, and the hatches could be taken off and put back. It had two masts.

"It's a ketch," said Maurice's father, who was sitting on the floor next to him. "Look at those lines! Some boat!"

"Will it really sail?" asked Jacob.

"It will," said Mr. Henry.

"Can we take it to the lake right now?" asked Maurice.

"Yes," said Mr. Henry. "But be very, very careful with it."

Maurice's mother smiled. "It's nice to see you so interested in something," she said to Maurice.

The two boys carried the boat to the park. They dropped their jackets on the grass and sat down on the cement ledge that ran all around the lake. Then they rigged the sails.

A brisk wind was blowing. Maurice and Jacob slid the boat into the water. Instantly, it raced toward the center of the lake, its sails puffed out with wind. The boys ran around to the other side, but Jacob suddenly stopped. His hair was blowing almost straight up.

"Come on!" shouted Maurice.

"Look!" said Jacob, pointing at the water. Two or three feet out from the shore, something glistened as the breeze lifted the water into small waves.

"Bedsprings," said Maurice.

"How can we get them?" asked Jacob.

Maurice sat down on the ground and took off his shoes and socks, but Jacob waded in after Maurice with his shoes on. The springs were heavy, and weeds were growing through them.

They dragged them onto the grass. Maurice put on his shoes and socks and jumped on the springs.

"We can borrow wire cutters from Mr. Klenk and make coils to put on our shoes."

"We can hook it up so it stretches across the room," said Jacob.

"I can pull it across the door so Patsy doesn't get through," said Maurice.

They picked up the springs and started home. Jacob's wet shoes squeaked.

Then Maurice stopped. "We forgot something," he said.

They dropped the springs and ran back to the lake. On the opposite side was the boat, its stern halfway up the cement ledge, its sails flapping.

"What are you going to tell them?" asked Jacob as they lifted the boat out of the water. The stern was smashed and the mainmast tilted.

"I don't know yet," answered Maurice.

"Could we say there was a little storm?"

"No, we'll have to tell them what really happened, that the boat went out of control," said Maurice.

"Because we weren't watching," said Jacob.

They put the boat on top of the springs; then with Maurice holding the front of the springs and Jacob the back, they started home.

At first, Maurice's father didn't say anything. Mrs. Henry told Jacob to go home and change his wet socks and shoes; then she went to the kitchen. Maurice heard her rattling pots and pans.

"If I had known you wanted bedsprings instead of a beautiful three-foot sailing ketch, I would have gotten you bedsprings," said Mr. Henry at last.

Maurice said nothing.

"Go to your room and think about what happened," said Mr. Henry.

Maurice put the sailboat under his bed next to the Victrola so he wouldn't have to look at it. He put a blanket on the bedsprings and sat down on them. One of the coils had come loose and was bobbing up beside him. He rested his arm on it.

He heard his parents talking the rest of the afternoon. His mother brought him a supper tray while it was still daylight.

Then Mr. Henry came and stood in Maurice's doorway. Maurice was still sitting on the springs.

"I have something to tell you," he said. "We have decided to move to the country as soon as school is over."

"How will I see Jacob?" asked Maurice.

"Jacob can take the bus. It's not very far. You can have a dog."

"Not Patsy!" asked Maurice.

"No," answered his father. "But your uncle has a racing bike he is going to give you. It's a little old, but it still goes."

"I'm sorry about the boat," said Maurice.

"Your mother and I are sorry too," said Mr. Henry. He came over and sat down next to Maurice on the bedsprings.

"They're still a little damp," he said.

Maurice gave him a corner of the blanket to sit on. They didn't speak about the sailboat. In fact, it was never mentioned again.

9. AN EXPLOSION

The Henrys moved to the country the day after school ended. Mrs. Henry said Maurice could take his collection if he could find something to pack it in. Mr. Klenk gave him an old steamer trunk with broken hinges. Jacob brought a length of rope to tie around it. Maurice was able to get everything into the trunk except the bedsprings. He gave them to Jacob.

The movers' truck drew up in front of Maurice's building around noon. Mr. Klenk, Jacob, and Maurice stood outside and watched the movers load the furniture on.

"I don't see how they can get all those things into the truck," said Jacob.

"They fit them together like a jigsaw puzzle," said Mr. Klenk.

The last items the movers brought down were Maurice's animals and his trunk. They placed the cages on the tops of bureaus at the front of the truck. They left the trunk at the back, near the tailgate.

"Can I ride in the truck with my things?" Maurice asked his father.

"If it's all right with the movers," said Mr. Henry.

Mr. Klenk waved his cigar at Maurice. "Come back and visit me," he said. "I'll keep an eye out for interesting things for your collection."

Jacob didn't say goodbye. He was coming out to visit the next day. He waved as Maurice hiked himself up onto the truck.

All the way through town, Maurice could see his mother and father driving behind in the rusty jeep they had bought for the country. But soon he lost sight of it as the truck pulled ahead.

Maurice walked to the front, winding through the furniture and crates, the boxes and baskets, to check up on his animals. The hamster was running on his wheel, but the robin, the snake, the lizard, and the salamanders were all asleep.

They turned off on a blacktop, then onto a dirt road. After that, the ride got bumpier. There were no buildings, no gasoline stations, no signs—only green hills and trees and birds sitting on telephone wires. Here and there a crumbling stone wall followed the curve of a hill. The sun was very warm, and the canvas curtains on either side of the truck's tailgate flapped back and forth.

All at once, there was a tremendous crash.

The furniture rattled, the cages danced on top of the bureaus, the robin chirped; and the pots banged against each other. They had driven over a big bump. Maurice's trunk teetered as they rounded a curve, then flew out, hit a rock, and seemed to explode into the air. Maurice saw his collection flying in all directions, then drop out of sight down the hill.

The truck stopped just as the jeep arrived. Maurice's father came running up to Maurice and lifted him down. Then everyone went to look over the hill. Maurice's things lay scattered everywhere among the rocks and tall grass. Maurice sat down on the road.

Mrs. Henry knelt beside him.

"Wow!" said Maurice. "Did you see that?"

Mrs. Henry stood up.

"The whole trunk blew up!" said Maurice. "It flew out in the air and exploded!"

"You can start a new collection," said Mr. Henry.

But Maurice didn't hear him. He was thinking that even the paper sacks of water he and Jacob had once dropped from the roof to the courtyard hadn't made such a terrific noise. He had never seen anything like it.

10. MAURICE'S BARN

Maurice's new room had one window and a slanted ceiling that was so low that Mr. and Mrs. Henry couldn't stand up straight beneath it.

When Maurice awoke the morning after the move, a branch was tapping against the windowpane and there were leaf-shaped shadows on the floor. Maurice wondered if he could step from the window to the big round branches of the tree that stood just outside. Just beyond the tree, Maurice could see a red barn. As he stared at it, a flock of birds flew from under the barn roof, circled in the sunlight, and flew back.

The room was empty except for Maurice's animals and his suitcase and the bed. The fields outside seemed empty too, except for the tall grass. The house was silent.

In the kitchen Maurice found a package of saltines and a glass of milk he had been too tired to finish the night before after all the unpacking.

Maurice's father walked in and sat down at the table. It was the same one that had been in Maurice's room in the city.

"Did you see the pump?" asked Mr. Henry.

"What's that?" asked Maurice.

"Sometimes there are storms, and the electricity goes off. Then you can use the hand pump to get water. It's just outside the door."

Maurice poked his finger into a little hole in the oilcloth.

"What do you think of the country?" asked Mr. Henry.

"It's okay," said Maurice.

"You are making a large hole in the oilcloth, Maurice. Why don't you take a look outside? Have you been to the barn?"

Maurice tried to balance four saltines against one other.

"Jacob will be here soon," said Mr. Henry. "You can take him to see the stream."

"What's in it?" asked Maurice.

"All right, Maurice," his father said, "you know what's in a stream!"

Maurice ate half a saltine. He wasn't very hungry.

"You'll get used to it here," said Mr. Henry. "It's new now. But you'll find lots of things to interest you."

At the word *things*, Maurice looked up at his father.

"There's nothing but grass," he said.

"Take a look in the barn," said Mr. Henry.

On his way out, Maurice tried the pump. He had to use both hands. Nothing happened for a moment; then a stream of cold bluish water gushed out on his feet. He squashed his way through the tall grass and the brambles to the barn.

The biggest door was padlocked, but next to it was a small door which hung half open from one hinge. He slipped inside.

He heard a great rustling of wings. For a moment he stood waiting for his eyes to get used to the dark. Then he looked straight up. The roof of the barn seemed miles above him. Small birds swooped through the rafters from which hung spider webs as big as trapeze nets. As soon as Maurice began to walk, an interesting musty smell arose from the floor. On his right were wooden stalls and on his left was an old hay wagon. One of its big wheels lay on the floor, half covered with hay. There were ladders of all sizes leaning up against the walls, and from the posts that supported the overhead rafters hung an extraordinary assortment of objects.

"Fish nets," said Maurice aloud. "A hoe, a rake, a bucket, another bucket, a bamboo pole with a line and three fish hooks, a dog collar, mousetraps, a leather jacket, a pitchfork, a lantern." There were many other things made out of leather or wood or metal, but he didn't know what they were.

A big shaft of sunlight fell across the floor. Maurice turned and saw his father standing in the doorway. Bits of hay and dust floated around him.

"Your mother has gone to get Jacob at the bus stop," he said.

Maurice noticed several lengths of chain and a tire tube hanging from a nail near the door.

"Do you like the barn?" asked Mr. Henry.

"Yes," said Maurice.

"That's where they used to keep the hay," said Mr. Henry, pointing to a platform above the wagon. "But I don't think we're going to have cows or horses." Just then Jacob came to the door. He was carrying a paper bag.

"Come in and see my barn," said Maurice.

Jacob stepped inside.

"What's in the bag?" asked Maurice.

"Jelly doughnuts and a wrench Mr. Klenk gave me to give to you."

Maurice cleared the hay off the rim of the wagon wheel, and they sat down to eat their doughnuts.

"Your mother said there was a stream we

could fish in," said Jacob.

"Not yet," said Maurice. "We have to fix up this barn. We have to find out what's in it. We can repair things. Like this wheel. We'll put it back on the wagon. Then, when we get too hot, we can go to the stream."

"What do we do first?" asked Jacob.

"First we have to find out the name of everything," said Maurice.

"Why?" asked Jacob.

"Because that's how you begin," answered Maurice. "Okay?"

"Okay," said Jacob.

ELEMENTS OF SHARED INQUIRY

A Short Course On Interpretive Reading And Discussion

PART THREE

INTERPRETIVE QUESTIONS IN THE FORM OF ISSUES

Quite apart from shared inquiry, we often talk about "issues". We find issues in the news, we argue about issues, and we agree or disagree with a political leader's stand on issues. In this sense, the word is used to describe any controversial problem about which people have different and usually opposite views. In shared inquiry, the word has a similar but more specialized meaning: an "issue" is an interpretive question that calls for alternative answers, one or both of which may turn out to be correct.

An issue may be an interpretive question that you can answer with either a "Yes" or "No". For example: Does the author want us to believe all of Toad's friends have faults? An issue may also be an interpretive question that requires you to choose between alternative ideas: Does the author want the reader to view Toad 1) as a child who never grew up *or* 2) as an animal trying to act like a human being?

As with all interpretive questions, you must back up your answer to a question in the form of an issue. You must show, with evidence from the story, why you decided on the "Yes" or "No" or why you chose one idea instead of the other. It is the support you present for either side of the issue that can increase our understanding of the selection.

An interpretive question in the form of an issue always contains a guess about the author's meaning. In our "Yes" and "No" question, the guess is: the author may want us to believe all of Toad's friends have faults. In the question with alternatives there are two guesses: 1) the author may want the reader to view Toad as a child who never grew up, or 2) the author may want the reader to view Toad as an animal trying to act like a human being.

Since many interpretive questions lead to alternative or opposing answers, you may wonder why we call your attention to questions in the form of issues. One reason is that issues are an excellent way to make the group immediately aware that a question can be answered correctly in more than one way. Often we don't realize this as quickly when we ask an interpretive question that does not contain a guess about the author's meaning. For example: Why did Toad tell the owners of the car who he was?

A second reason is that a question in the form of an issue is a good way to interest someone in a problem of interpretation. In this respect, questions as issues serve much the same purpose in shared inquiry that they serve in debate. They dramatize a problem by making people wonder which side will have the stronger case. In another respect, however, issues in shared inquiry differ from issues in debate. Our interest is not primarily in proving one side right and the other side wrong or in having some participants stick to the side they first think is right, even though they change their minds later. Often, participants discover that the truth about the author's meaning consists of good ideas from both sides. Nevertheless, the issue has served its purpose if it captures the attention of the participants who are discussing it.

When you try to write questions in the form of issues, there are three mistakes that are easy to make. The first is to present an issue that really can't be answered in two alternative or opposing ways if you have read the whole selection carefully. For example: Will Toad and his friends recapture Toad Hall from the Wild Wooders? The question is an issue only for someone who has not finished the selection or has read it carelessly.

A second mistake is to present an issue that possibly can be answered in two ways, but almost all of the evidence from the selection is on one side. For us such a question would be: Is Toad conceited? At the very end of "The Wind in the Willows", Toad acts more modestly, but throughout most of the story he praises himself.

A final mistake is to make an issue out of the group's beliefs instead of the author's meaning—in other words, to ask an evaluative question instead of an interpretive one: Did you feel sorry for Toad when he was imprisoned?

To avoid all the mistakes we have mentioned, remember that an issue is satisfactory in shared inquiry only when you think it can be answered in opposing or alternative ways based on a careful reading of the whole selection.

EXERCISE 6

"All Summer in a Day"

Place an (Is) next to each question that is in the form of an issue. These are *interpretive* questions that call for alternative answers based on a careful reading of the story. Place an (X) next to each question that is not an issue. Hint: Not every good interpretive question is an issue.

____ 1. Does the author want us to believe Margot is the only child unhappy on Venus?

____ 2. Why does the author describe the children as being "Like so many roses, so many weeds, intermixed . . ."?

____ 3. Could you adjust to living in a place like Venus?

____ 4. Does the author have the children lock Margot in the closet mainly to show how cruel they can be or how ignorant they are of the pleasures of the sun?

____ 5. Apart from the rain, does the author present Venus as an unattractive place?

____ 6. Will Margot go back to Earth?

____ 7. Does the author want us to believe the Earth has become an undesirable place to live?

____ 8. Do you remember things you saw when you were two?

____ 9. Is Margot different from the other children because she remembers the sun or because she has more need of it?

____10. Why does the author include different descriptions of the sun in the children's dreams, in what they read, and in Margot's poem?

FOLLOW-UP QUESTIONS

To explore an interpretive question successfully in discussion, you must use follow-up questions. These are all the questions the leaders or participants ask after the interpretive question for discussion has been stated. The purpose of follow-up questions is to encourage you and all participants to think for yourselves and, at the same time, to use what is said to keep the discussion moving until the interpretive question is answered, or time runs out.

This is not easy to do. Some participants talk so fast that it is hard to think about what they are saying. At times, you will hear more ideas than you can possibly think about, and at other times, no one will have anything to say. Ideas are often expressed in ways that are not immediately clear. You will discover that some of your fellow participants are quicker to offer opinions than to support them with facts, and sometimes the facts they do offer are incorrect. Some participants will talk about topics not related to the interpretive question or even to the selection; and you may from time to time lose your own train of thought. The effective use of follow-up questions by the discussion leaders—and by you as a participant—will help to handle all these situations and to keep the group's attention on the interpretive question.

Follow-up questions have four uses: to get participants to answer interpretive questions; to clarify their answers; to ask participants to support their opinions with facts; and to keep discussion on the track.

1. When a participant fails to answer an opening interpretive question or any interpretive question, the discussion leaders repeat the question to the same participant or to someone else. They may also rephrase the question, say the same thing in different words. Example: Mary, why does the Pied Piper tell the Mayor and the Corporation that he uses his charm chiefly on creatures that do people harm? Rephrasing: Howard, in talking to the town leaders, why does the Pied Piper emphasize the power of his pipe to get rid of animals that the people don't want around? Another way the discussion leaders may handle a lack of response is to ask a factual or evaluative question that may give you some ideas that will help you to answer their interpretive question. Question: Tom, why does Browning contrast the appearance of the Mayor and the Pied Piper? Answer: I don't know. Question: Tom, how are the Mayor and the Pied Piper dressed?

   So far, in talking about the use of follow-up questions to get responses, we have presented situations in which you and other participants offer no answer at all. Follow-up questions are also asked to get more than one answer to an interpretive question. Examples: Alice, do you agree with Ted? Bob, how would you answer the question? Fran, what do you think? Even when it turns out that two participants have the same interpretation, asking for additional opinions is not wasted. The second participant often produces new facts to support the opinion.
2. The second use of follow-up questions is to clarify answers. The discussion leaders and the participants should ask for clarification of any response that they

don't understand. You can almost always be sure that if *you* don't understand what is said, at least some other members of the group don't either. One way to get clarification is to ask the participant to repeat what he or she said in different words. Examples: Sally, could you restate that? Frank, what did you mean by that? Another way is to state in your own words what you *think* the participant means and ask him or her if you are correct. Example: John, are you saying that you believe the townspeople are as much to blame for the loss of the children as the Mayor and the Corporation?

3. The third use of follow-up questions is *to ask participants to support their opinions with facts.* This is done by asking factual questions that require participants to read from the selection or to put what the author said into their own words. Examples: Where do you see that in the story? What evidence can you find in the story for that statement? Everyone has a right to an opinion, but what makes some opinions better than others is the way they are backed up with evidence from the story.
4. The final use of follow-up questions is to keep discussion on the track. It takes a great deal of concentration on the part of both leaders and participants to stick to the interpretive problem being discussed. Therefore, it is not uncommon to find participants and leaders occasionally wandering into other areas of discussion about either the selection or their personal experience. The solution in both cases is to ask interpretive or factual questions that bring the group back to the problem of meaning which they are supposed to be discussing. Example: Why did the Mayor and the Cor-

poration offer the Piper fifty thousand guilders when he only asked for one thousand? Answer: I don't know how much a guilder is worth, but I would have offered anything to get rid of rats. I've hated them since I saw the movie, *Ben*. Question: Do you think the Mayor and his council offered so much because they didn't expect to pay the Pied Piper anything?

EXERCISE 7

"The Pied Piper of Hamelin"

Each sequence below consists of a question and an answer. After each response, write one follow-up question. Your question should continue the discussion of the poem by taking into account the participant's answer *and* the leader's question.

1. Leader: Why is the Pied Piper dressed in "quaint attire"?
   Participant: I don't know.
   Your question: ____________________

2. Leader: Why does the poet have the Pied Piper lead the children into the mountain instead of into the water?
   Participant: He wants to teach the people in the town a lesson, but he doesn't want to hurt the children.
   Your question: ____________________

3. Leader: Why does the author have one rat and one child left?
   Participant: To show the Pied Piper's magic isn't perfect.
   Your question: ____________________

4. Leader: Why was the Pied Piper willing to accept payment in food from the Head Cook?
   Participant: Because he had got money from the Caliph.

Your question: ______________________________

5. Leader: Before he rid the town of the rats, why didn't the Pied Piper warn the Mayor he would take away the children if he wasn't paid?

Participant: A hint is enough.

Your question: ______________________________

6. Leader: Why did the townspeople want the world to know what had happened?

Participant: I wouldn't have. When something sad happens to me I want to keep quiet and forget it.

Your question: ______________________________

RESOLUTION IN SHARED INQUIRY

In shared inquiry, the word "resolution" means more than getting the right answer to a question.

Resolution is that point in a discussion when all the members of your group could, if called upon, (1) answer the interpretive question on which the discussion is based in their own way, and (2) support their answers with facts from the selection. Since interpretive questions can usually be answered satisfactorily in more than one way, it is likely that members of the group will have different answers.

You can see from this definition that resolution does not mean total agreement or even a majority opinion about an answer. Resolution is an individual matter. *It occurs when you are convinced that the way in which you would answer an interpretive question could be supported with evidence that satisfies you.* If you were the discussion leader, you should continue to explore the interpretive question at least until you could make up your own mind about how the question should be answered. As a participant, you should feel free to bring up points about an interpretive question as long as you have any doubt about how *you* would answer it.

One reliable sign that the group is leaving an interpretive question before everyone has resolved it to his or her satisfaction is the attempt of a participant to reintroduce it if the leaders switch to another question about the author's meaning. If that occurs, your discussion leaders should backtrack for a moment or two to determine whether new facts or ideas are being raised that could provide another answer to the question you are discussing.

There are also signs to show that you are approaching the resolution of an interpretive question or that it probably will not be worthwhile to continue the discussion of it much longer: the group begins to repeat itself, to take up minor points, and to wander away from the question. When that happens, the group has probably run out of ideas that further the exploration of the interpretive question on which this segment of your discussion is based.

Because resolution depends so much on what the leaders and the participants do, the same interpretive question might be answered differently by different groups. Your group might answer the question about why the author has Maurice's trunk explode on the way to the country by talking about Maurice's fascination with the explosion, his inability to take an interest in the country as an alternative to his collection of things, and then the opportunity the explosion gives him to start a whole new collection in the barn. Another group may have answers to the same question that never occurred to your group. They might mention how the explosion allows the author to show that Mr. Henry is sympathetic to Maurice's feelings and that he planned the move to the country not to stop Maurice from collecting things but to replace his room with the barn.

Although your group should try to resolve in its own way every interpretive question they are discussing before proceeding to the next one, the success of shared inquiry does not depend wholly on whether you do or not. You can increase your understanding of a selection even if you feel more could be said in answer to some interpretive questions. You can also experience with each interpretive question the pleasure of thinking for yourself.

EXERCISE 8

"Maurice's Room"

The purpose of this exercise is to illustrate what we mean by resolution and to test our statement that resolution of an interpretive question will be different for different groups. Your discussion leaders will divide you into two or three small groups and ask a member of each group to list all the topics or ideas you would have to discuss to answer the question:

> Why would Maurice rather collect things than do anything else?